MW00476097

Cleaning is Murder

A Myrtle Clover Cozy Mystery, Volume 13

Elizabeth Spann Craig

Published by Elizabeth Spann Craig, 2018.

CLEANING IS MURDER

First edition. August 4, 2018.

Written by Elizabeth Spann Craig.

In memory of Mamma and Amma.

Chapter One

"You're slipping," said Myrtle in irritation as Miles carefully placed tiles to spell 'too' on the Scrabble board. "And you even used up one of your blank tiles."

Miles gave his friend a sour look. He shouted, "That's because it's noisy in here. It plays havoc with my concentration."

As if to corroborate his words, the vacuum cleaner, in the hands of Myrtle's housekeeper Puddin, swerved perilously close to his feet. It nearly knocked over the card table where Myrtle and Miles had set up their game.

"That Puddin," said Myrtle, glaring at her housekeeper. "She was supposed to be here hours ago. I didn't plan on her interrupting our game. She's a terror with the vacuum."

Miles shouted, "Couldn't you send her away? Have her come back later?"

"You know she'd *never* come back," said Myrtle. "And my house is a disaster."

Miles stood up. "Let's move the game to my house. It's quiet there."

"Absolutely not. All the tiny tiles would fly off the board and mess up the whole game," said Myrtle.

1

Miles looked as if that thought very much appealed to him. But then, he wasn't winning. "I'll be careful."

Puddin took another menacing pass at them with the vacuum, her pasty, doughy face sullen but focused.

Miles carefully placed both hands on either side of the Scrabble board and lifted it while Myrtle scowled at him. Then he crept toward Myrtle's front door, focused on the tiles on the board the entire time. When he reached the front door, he turned and said loudly, "It's fine. I've got it."

Myrtle said, "Well, don't try to open that door." She reluctantly stood up.

Miles, however, in a fit of overconfidence, hooked his arm under the board and reached for the door handle with his other hand. In flew Myrtle's feral cat, Pasha, unnoticed by Miles, who was still delivering his undivided attention to the Scrabble tiles. Pasha belatedly spotted Puddin and the vacuum—two nemeses. She gave a hissing scream right as Puddin switched off the vacuum. Puddin, never a fan of Pasha, screamed too. Miles jumped wildly, tiles scattered everywhere, and the word game crashed to the floor as Pasha leapt back out the front door.

Myrtle walked over and stared at the floor with disgust. "So much for our game." She turned to Puddin. "Puddin, you're a danger to society with that vacuum."

Puddin put her hands on her hips. "You said you wanted your floor cleaned."

"That's enough of your foolishness, Puddin. You're a disaster today. The carpet looks all right ... just move on to the bathroom, would you?" said Myrtle.

Miles put the Scrabble board back on the table and dumped handfuls of tiles on top. "Let's start over."

"Certainly not! The only reason that you want to start the game over is because you were losing, Miles. My memory is excellent and I can picture where every word was. We'll reconstruct the game."

Miles looked glumly at the pile of tiles. "It will take longer to do that than it would be simply to start over again."

"As if you have anything else to do! I happen to know there's nothing on your agenda for the rest of the day," said Myrtle.

Miles turned a few tiles over. "And how do you know that?"

"You told me, yourself. You said you were going to have to find something to do. So we have all the time in the world to put the game back the way it was," said Myrtle.

The sound of shampoo bottles and other paraphernalia hitting the floor and the bottom of the bathtub came from the direction of the bathroom. Puddin muttered darkly to herself in the back.

Myrtle's doorbell rang, and she lifted her eyebrows. "Who on earth could that be?" She stood up and walked to the front door, opening it.

Her son, Red, was standing there, frowning. "Where's your cane, Mama? Did you walk all the way across your living room without it?"

"You may be the police chief of this town, Red, but you're not the cane police," said Myrtle with a sniff. "I don't need a cane inside my own house. I could navigate my living room blindfolded."

"Let's not give that theory a try," said Red, shuddering. He stepped inside. "Hi, Miles. Everything going okay with you?"

"Aside from a bad bout of Scrabble? I suppose so," said Miles.

Red shook his head. "I can tell you where you went wrong. You went wrong when you agreed to play Scrabble with Mama. You've heard of card sharks? She's a tile shark."

Myrtle glared daggers at him. "You make it sound as though I'm cheating—keeping an extra 'T' in my pocket or something."

"You cheat by playing without a handicap," said Red. "When you play Scrabble, you should be given all Js and Qs. Or only vowels. Otherwise, it's unfair."

"Thanks for your misguided concern about our game. As it happens, we were having lots of fun until you arrived. Weren't we, Miles?" asked Myrtle.

Miles's face was dubious.

Red said, "It looks like somebody got mad and flung all the tiles off the board."

"Oh, that was Puddin's fault. She's a holy terror today," said Myrtle.

Red snorted. "Worse than usual?"

"You wouldn't think it was funny if she were throwing around *your* things and messing up *your* game with a vacuum," said Myrtle. "Anyway, why are you here? Did you come by to drive me up the wall?"

Red shook his head. "Actually, I was just stopping by to see if you had anything to eat over here."

Miles gasped so violently that he gave himself the hiccups. It was quite a loud case of the hiccups, too. Red grinned at him. "It's okay to eat *prepared* food here, Miles."

Myrtle frowned at Miles and said to Red, "I have a whole kitchen full of food. Help yourself. But don't you have food at your own house?"

"*That* is a matter of opinion," said Red, walking toward the kitchen.

Miles hiccupped again and followed Red, pouring himself a glass of water.

Myrtle said, "Elaine thinks it's food and you don't?"

"Precisely. My dear wife's gone all granola on me. House is full of sprouts and chia seeds and all kinds of crazy stuff." He shook his head as he rummaged in Myrtle's refrigerator.

Miles took a large gulp of water and said in a steady voice, "I wondered what made you choose your mother's house for sustenance."

A look passed between Red and Miles and Miles hiccupped again.

Myrtle said crossly, "Miles, you're being obstreperous today. You know I have food here. I cooked just last night, and it was superb. It was so good that when I was putting my leftovers away, I thought it was such a pity that no one else lived here and could enjoy it."

Red blurted, "That's great Mama, but I was only looking for a sandwich. I'm still on duty and a casserole would make me too sleepy this afternoon."

"I never said it was a casserole" said Myrtle, narrowing her eyes.

Red drawled, "With you, it's *always* a casserole."

Myrtle watched in annoyance as Red took the rest of her ham and mayonnaise and put together two large sandwiches. "I don't understand why you're not grabbing lunch on the go at a fast food place or something."

Miles said thoughtfully, "I bet Elaine packs his lunch every day."

Red pointed at Miles. "Good analytical thinking. You should join the force. Elaine has been sending me to work with all sorts of organic, non-GMO mumbo-jumbo. She's gone vegan, too, and I don't like the slice of 'cheese' that she puts in my sandwich. If it's not dairy, I'm not sure what it is. The sandwich bread is some kind of multigrain, gluten-free obscenity. She offered me a coconut milk yogurt for a snack. But I can't pick up fast food because she'd know I wasn't eating her food if I'm spending money on lunch. This is a delicate situation."

"Elaine's hobbies never last for long," said Miles in a comforting tone and finally without hiccupping.

"That's right. She gets these short-term obsessions and then she's done," said Myrtle.

"I sure hope you're right," said Red. He enthusiastically chewed and swallowed a large bite of his sandwich. "I can barely choke down the food she gives me every night. And I really hate that. I've always tried not to hurt her feelings when she embarks on these madcap hobbies. I've been able to sustain an interest in her art, landscaping, knitting, photography, and a lot of other stuff."

Myrtle said thoughtfully, "And, for the most part, you've done a good job acting interested."

"This one is really testing me. You should have seen what she gave me to eat last night. It makes me feel nauseated just thinking about it," said Red with a shiver.

Myrtle said, "It couldn't have been that bad."

Red said, "Mama, you know I'm not exactly your biggest fan when it comes to your cooking."

"For whatever unwarranted reason," said Myrtle coldly.

Miles smiled.

"Well, let's just say that I'd rather have eaten the entirety of whatever casserole you concocted than what Elaine put on the table last night," said Red.

Miles stared at him, shocked into silence by this statement.

Red said, "Fortunately, Jack had the foresight to try and flush one of his shoes down the toilet and Elaine had to run away from the table. While she was in the back of the house, I stuffed the abomination down in the bottom of the trashcan and concealed it with trash."

Miles said in wonder, "What *was* this awful meal?"

"It was some sort of soggy gluten-free wrap stuffed with limp veggies and held together with hummus. It fell apart when I looked at it." Red took a final, appreciative bite of his last ham sandwich. "Then this morning it was tofu scramble. And I was so hungry I thought I might cry."

Miles said, "Do you have a long-range plan for handling this? You can't just not eat."

"I know. I've lost a ton of weight already. I'll waste away," said Red, alarming himself by his own words.

Myrtle snorted. "I see no wasting away in your immediate future, Red. But listen: while Elaine is in this healthy mode, why not stockpile food over here? You could do some grocery shopping for both of us. Then you can fib to Elaine and say you need to run by and check on me for whatever reason."

Red rolled his eyes. "It's no lie that I need to check up on you. Okay, that sounds like a plan. I'll go on a big shopping trip later today and tell Elaine that I'm giving you a hand. I just hope she doesn't find out. She's so *earnest*. Elaine thinks she's doing this good deed to make Jack and me healthier. I feel bad about not eating her food because she's worked so hard at it."

Miles said, "She's put *Jack* on that food?"

"Well, she's tried. But it's not exactly easy to make a nearly three-year-old eat carrot cake protein bars. Jack has gone on a hunger strike. I slip him Cheerios when I can," said Red. "I'll try to rescue him later for a stroller ride and maybe we'll walk to Bo's Diner and get some real food. And I'll pay in cash so Elaine won't find out."

There was a crash in the bedroom and the sound of books falling out of the bookcase. This was followed by more dire mutterings from Puddin.

Red said, "She *is* bad today. What's going on with her?" He walked over to Myrtle's pantry and grabbed the potato chips.

Myrtle shrugged. "I assumed at first that Dusty was getting on her nerves. But then she mentioned shortly after she arrived that it had something to do with someone who owed her money."

Red raised his eyebrows. "Puddin is in a sound enough financial position to lend people money?" He grabbed a handful of chips from the bag and stuffed them in his mouth.

"No, this seemed to be someone she worked for. She launched into a long explanation, but Miles and I were about to play our game and I needed her to clean, not flap her gums. I'm sure I'll get to the bottom of it later." Myrtle paused and hollered, "Puddin, in case it's not completely obvious to you, you need to pick those books up!"

"Stupid books!" came the angry and tearful reply.

"I'll leave you to it," said Red quickly. "Good luck." He started to put away the chips, then shook the bag. "Not enough in here to put away. I'll take them with me."

Myrtle sighed. "When are you going on this grocery shopping expedition? I'll need some food in the house now that you've raided my pantry and fridge."

"I'll go this afternoon. Anything you specifically want? I'll try and keep my stash separate." Red walked toward the front door.

"Yes. Don't you need to write it down?"

"Nope. Mind's like a steel trap." Red tapped his head.

Myrtle frowned doubtfully as she followed him to the front door. "Hm. I need one percent milk. *Not* two percent. And I want brown eggs, *not* white eggs. And I'd like a bag of barbeque potato chips ... *not* any other kind."

"Got it," said Red. "See you, Miles." Red turned at the door and gave her a stern look. "Mama, you aren't using your cane."

Myrtle bared her teeth at him.

"When I come back with those groceries, I want to see you holding that cane," said Red firmly as he shut the door behind him.

"I'll hold that cane, all right ... so I can beat him with it," growled Myrtle.

"Assaulting a police officer?" asked Miles, returning to the living room and sitting down at the card table. "I have a feeling that may backfire on you."

"All right then, perhaps a more visual display of my displeasure is in order," said Myrtle.

Miles raised an eyebrow. "In the form of an army of gnomes? Facing his house?"

"It's ridiculous that those precious yard gnomes upset Red so badly. They're so whimsical. All I need is for Dusty to come by and give me a hand with them and we'll be all set," said Myrtle.

"Are you certain that you want to make Red angry *before* he goes to the grocery store and buys you food?" asked Miles.

"Red will botch that, anyway. Even when I'd send him to the store when he was a little boy he'd come back with the wrong stuff. I'd tell him to get green apples and by-golly, he'd come home with red ones. I'd ask him to get Duke's mayonnaise and do you know what he'd come back with?"

"Mustard? Ketchup?" asked Miles, hazarding a guess. He continued putting tiles back on the board.

"Even worse. *Hellman's* mayonnaise! It's as if he wasn't even listening to me at all," said Myrtle.

"It does sound like a habitual problem," agreed Miles. "But I will point out that Red is now in his 40s. Perhaps he'll come back with exactly the eggs and milk you want."

"Let's say it's extremely unlikely. He was way too smug when he said that he didn't need to write a list to remember the items.

I'll enjoy reminding him of that fact when he comes here with whole milk and white eggs. Putting the gnomes out will protest the cane issue *and* the messing up my grocery order issue. Two birds with one stone," said Myrtle. "Now to find out where that Dusty is today. Puddin!"

A tearful and still sullen Puddin appeared reluctantly from the back.

Myrtle looked at her in alarm. "What's happened now?"

"Stupid knickknacks," snarled Puddin, holding out her hands to reveal a broken vase.

Myrtle put her hands on her hips. "All right. What's going on with you, Puddin? You're even worse today than usual."

To Myrtle's surprise and horror, Puddin burst into tears.

Chapter Two

Miles pretended to be so completely absorbed in arranging tiles back on the Scrabble board that he didn't notice.

Myrtle sighed, located a tissue box, and thrust it at Puddin. "What in heaven's name is wrong? Clearly this has nothing to do with knickknacks and books."

Puddin sulked through her tears. "Them didn't help, though."

"Whatever," said Myrtle. "Now what's going on?"

Puddin said vindictively, "Havin' a bad day. Yer creepy friend called me this morning."

"Creepy friend? Erma? And if you *do* mean Erma, please cease and desist using the word 'friend' to describe her." Myrtle shuddered. Erma, her vile next-door neighbor, was most decidedly not a friend.

"Naw! That witch." Puddin gave her a scornful look.

"Wanda? She called *you*?" Myrtle and Miles exchanged glances.

Miles said, "How did she even know your phone number?"

Myrtle said, "You're not paying attention again, Miles. Wanda is a *psychic*." She turned back to Puddin. "What did she say to you?"

Puddin angrily swiped an errant tear off her cheek. "Said I was in danger."

"Sounds likely," agreed Miles. "Those words represent ninety percent of what constitutes conversation from Wanda."

Puddin gave him a blank look.

"Miles means that Wanda frequently warns people they're in danger. Usually me. But I'm still around, aren't I? What else did she say?" asked Myrtle.

"Nothin'. I slammed down the phone," said Puddin.

"Avoidance. Your usual strategy for dealing with life's unpleasantries. Well, I can't imagine that a two-minute phone conversation with Wanda is responsible for this display of emotion," said Myrtle.

She waited while Puddin blew her nose and appeared to be trying to decide how much she wanted to share with Myrtle. Puddin finally spat out, "It's that Amos Subers."

Miles lifted his eyebrows. "I know Amos."

"What about Amos? Do you clean for him?" asked Myrtle.

Puddin said, "Not for long, if he don't pay me."

Myrtle said, "Not pay you? For how long?"

"For the past month. No money!" Puddin made a wild motion with her hand intended to depict abject destitution.

Myrtle said, "Hm. Well, that probably means that he only owes you for one cleaning. You're not exactly consistent with your housekeeping, are you? Amos doesn't look the sort to put up with any shenanigans, either."

Puddin curled her lip. "Ain't been no shenanigans. I done cleaned for him. He owes me money!"

Miles cleared his throat as he carefully arranged tiles on the gameboard. "Have you broached the topic in a professional manner?"

Puddin gave him an uncomprehending stare and then turned to Myrtle for a translation. "How did you ask him for the money, Puddin? Did you screech at him that he owed you? Or did you mail him a bill with a deadline for payment?"

Puddin's eyes narrowed. "Told him upfront. Ain't scared of him!"

"What did he tell you? Is he planning on paying you?" asked Myrtle.

"He's cheap," said Puddin in disgust. "Said he'd pay me 'next time.' When I go in there 'next time,' he's going to be sorry if my money ain't there!"

Miles asked, "When *is* the next time?"

"After I finish here," said Puddin. "That's what's got me keyed up." She heaved a deep, unsteady breath.

Myrtle said, "All right. If you don't get your money this morning, call me and I'll go over and argue your case. He can't continue expecting you to clean without remuneration."

Puddin's eyes narrowed suspiciously, "Don't like it when you don't speak English."

"You won't work if he won't pay," clarified Myrtle. "Just call me."

Puddin glanced around Myrtle's house. "We done here? Looks clean."

"Does it?" asked Myrtle.

"Looks better than it did before I got here," said Puddin.

"That's a matter of opinion. There was a lot of crashing and breaking going on back there. You apparently have too much on your mind to focus on what you're doing. Luckily for you, I want to reconstruct my Scrabble game with Miles. You can go ahead and head out," said Myrtle, sitting down at the card table.

A few minutes later, Puddin stomped to the front door.

"And *don't* take my cleaning supplies," said Myrtle.

"Them is mine," said Puddin, giving Myrtle a dour look.

"They certainly aren't. I've taken care to mark my cleaning bottles with a Sharpie pen. See?" Myrtle pointed to the bottles. The cleaning bottles *'property of Myrtle Clover'* written on them in large lettering.

Puddin said, "But if I don't take them to his house, there won't be nothing there for me to clean with! Mr. Subers don't buy cleaning supplies. He has this glass bottle of stinky home-made junk."

"Making his own cleaning supplies sounds like strikingly good judgment on his part. I should adopt his reasoning and follow his lead," said Myrtle. "Honestly, Puddin. Go ahead and take the multi-purpose bottle but bring it back the next time you come."

Puddin slouched out the door.

"Good riddance," said Myrtle. "Now, where were we?"

Miles said, "You were going to ask Puddin if Dusty could come over here today and pull out gnomes to irritate Red."

Myrtle's eyes grew big and this time she did grab her cane, but only to help her navigate the front porch and walkway. She hurried out and yelled, "Puddin!" but Puddin had driven away.

Myrtle walked back inside. "Missed her. Pooh."

"Why don't you call her cell phone?" asked Miles.

"Because half the time she doesn't pay the bill and it's out of service. The other half the phone stays cooped up in her glove compartment with a dead battery," said Myrtle. "Calling her house phone is usually the only way to reach her, but we know she's not at home. There has been entirely too much aggravation today. This was intended to be a peaceful morning. I was to start off with a clean house via an energized and focused Puddin."

Miles snorted at Myrtle's fantastical vision.

"Then you and I would play a competitive game of Scrabble where I would pull off a difficult but well-deserved win," continued Myrtle.

Miles pushed his glasses up his nose and said defensively, "I was doomed from the start. My letters were horrible."

Myrtle said, "And my son wasn't supposed to drop by to eat all my food and chastise me for not using my cane. All in all, it's been a most unsatisfactory day."

"Well, let's see if we can hit the reset button," said Miles. "You need to cool down. Remember what you said the last time your day got hijacked like this?"

"That I wanted to open a bottle of sherry?"

"No, that you needed to find a way to start over your day and get back into a good mood," said Miles.

"I said that?" asked Myrtle, frowning. "That doesn't sound like something I'd say."

"You were quite explicit about it. It was made in the tone of someone who was making a resolution," said Miles.

"Are you sure I wasn't planning a *revolution* instead of a resolution? That sounds far more likely," said Myrtle.

Miles shook his head. "Come on. I've got the board set up exactly as it was before."

Myrtle sighed. "All right. Let me see how well you've managed to resurrect this game." She sat down at the table and stared at the board. "Miles, this is all wrong."

Miles narrowed his eyes. "I meticulously reconstructed the game."

"You're remembering words from the *last* game we played," said Myrtle.

"From two weeks ago? I doubt it," said Miles coldly.

"You most certainly are. And you were in a much better position in that game. The words today were actually like *this*." And Myrtle proceeded to rearrange tiles until they fit her vision of the game in progress.

Miles stared at the board. "You're delusional."

"*You* are," said Myrtle, but further arguments were cut short by the doorbell ringing.

"It's Grand Central Station today," grumbled Myrtle, heading to the front door.

"Remember, you're hitting the reset button on your day," said Miles.

She pulled the door open to see a gaunt woman with leathery skin. A shabby yellow top hung on her emaciated frame and she offered Myrtle a smile, revealing a hodgepodge of missing and crooked teeth.

"Wanda!" said Myrtle, standing back so that the psychic could come inside. "We were just talking about you a few minutes ago."

Wanda nodded as if that went without saying. She glanced around the living room and slumped. "She's already gone," she said with a gusty sigh.

"Puddin? Yes, a few minutes ago," said Myrtle. "But she mentioned that you called her this morning. I think you shook her up. But she was rattled already, so who knows?" She saw Wanda eyeing the kitchen and said, "Come on in and let's find you some ... lunch? Brunch? Whatever meal it is."

"Hi Wanda," said Miles.

Myrtle noted that Miles sounded quite cordial. Perhaps he'd finally gotten over the fact that Wanda was a cousin of his. He continued to feel a good deal of financial responsibility for her, however, and frequently gave her gifts to help her survive. The psychic business was apparently not thriving in Bradley, North Carolina.

Wanda gave Miles a nod in greeting. "Got something to tell you."

Miles looked discomfited. "I'm in danger?" he asked, his voice pitched slightly higher than usual.

"Nope. Love that houseplant you gave me." Wanda gave her big grin again.

"It's still alive?" Miles looked stunned. The shack that Wanda called home was not designed to allow living things to thrive. Including Wanda.

Wanda said, "Sure is. Makes me want to grow more stuff."

"Don't you and Dan have a garden already?" asked Myrtle, opening her pantry doors and gazing critically at the food inside.

Wanda shrugged a bony shoulder. "Fer food. Tomatoes and such. Not fer fun."

Miles said, "So you're thinking about planting flowers and shrubs and things like that?"

He exchanged a look with Myrtle. It would be humanly impossible to beautify the house Wanda shared with her brother, Crazy Dan. It was totally covered with hubcaps and the hubcaps were for sale. They were, fortunately, slow sellers so the house still retained its protective exterior. The yard, if it could really be called a yard since it doubled as a parking lot, was red clay and not a speck of grass dared to grow there.

Wanda shrugged again. "Maybe. Or maybe herbs or somethin."

Myrtle snapped her fingers. "You should be my guest at the garden club gala in a week!"

Miles's eyes grew wide.

Wanda drawled, "Gala?" trying out the unfamiliar word on her tongue.

"Yes. My garden club that I've been part of for over fifty years is having a gala this year to raise money for a new town park. I'm supposed to be selling tickets and it would be a relief if I had to sell one fewer. I've already made Miles buy one," said Myrtle.

Miles's face offered glum affirmation of the fact.

"There'll be a special speaker who'll give a talk to beginners about improving their yards. And there'll be lots and lots of *food*.

And let me tell you—those ladies pick at their food like birds. We can send you home with the gala's leftovers and it should feed you and Dan for a week."

Wanda considered this for a second and then her eyes crinkled in a smile as she nodded.

"Good. Then that's settled."

Miles looked at Myrtle. He would likely talk with her later about the odd combination of the garden club gala and the attendance of Wanda the Psychic.

Myrtle pulled out a can of soup. Red had apparently finished her loaf of bread, but Wanda could eat some canned potato and broccoli soup and have peanut butter crackers. "How is your decluttering project going? You really got rid of a lot of stuff."

Wanda shook her head sadly. "Dan brought *in* a lot of stuff. We're the same as we ever was."

Which meant that you couldn't see the surfaces of any tables and some of the floor.

Wanda plopped down in a kitchen chair and a few minutes later Myrtle produced the soup and crackers.

Miles said, "So you apparently knew something bad about Puddin. With the ... psychic thing."

Myrtle rolled her eyes. Miles never sounded so awkward as when he was trying to wrap his head around Wanda's gifts.

"Knew somethin' bad was goin' to *happen* to her." Wanda put her thin face close to the bowl, apparently not wanting to lose a single drop, and quickly and accurately shoveled potato soup in her mouth.

"Okay," said Miles. "And so you called her."

Myrtle interjected, "And Puddin didn't want to take the call."

Wanda nodded, already halfway finished with the soup.

"So you came here. Looking for Puddin," said Miles. "Because you knew she'd be here?"

"She has the sight, Miles. For heaven's sake," said Myrtle impatiently.

"Was goin' to be able to see her, too. Left in plenty of time. But the car broke down on the way," said Wanda. She started in on the crackers.

This was an entirely likely scenario. Another feature of the property where Wanda lived was the metal graveyard of cars, in various stages of decomposition, around the perimeter. Most of them were on concrete blocks, but from time to time, Crazy Dan would get one of them working for a short period, although never very reliably.

"We can take you back home," said Miles. "We'll walk to my house and I'll take you back myself."

Wanda's living conditions appalled Miles and seemed to make him guilty that he led such a comfortable life while she struggled. Although her struggles never seemed to make Wanda suffer—she simply accepted them as she did her gift and everything else, straightforwardly.

"Thanks. But I need to stay here for a little while first," said Wanda.

"Of course you may," said Myrtle immediately. "You may stay here as long as you like."

Wanda gave her a smile. "It's just that Puddin is goin' to call. Thought I'd stay fer that."

Which is when Myrtle's phone rang.

Chapter Three

Myrtle frowned and picked up the phone. "Hello?"

There was a screech on the other end and Myrtle pulled the phone away from her ear. The screeching went on for another minute. When there was a pause, she cautiously put the phone back to her ear. "Puddin?" she asked.

There was more screeching on the other end.

Myrtle finally shouted into the phone, "Puddin! I can't understand you."

Wanda calmly rose from the kitchen table and carefully pushed her chair underneath the table.

"Come over!" yelled Puddin.

"Where?" asked Myrtle. "Are you still at the Subers house?"

"Yes! An' he's *dead*!" Puddin spat out the last word as if Subers had arranged it as a personal affront to her.

Myrtle hung up and said, "Miles, can you drive us?"

Miles sighed. "Are we sure that Puddin knows what she's talking about? It would be humiliating if we were to discover that Amos Subers is merely taking a well-deserved late-morning nap."

"Through all that yelling?" asked Myrtle.

23

"Perhaps a mild stroke?" suggested Miles.

Wanda shook her head. "He's dead, all right."

Miles hurried home to get his car and then drove quickly over to Amos Subers' house. Myrtle grasped the passenger side door as Miles speedily took a turn. Wanda sat stoically in the back seat.

"Shouldn't you call Red?" asked Miles. "In the off-chance that this *is* an emergency?"

Myrtle said, "Why on earth would I do that? A dead person hardly constitutes an emergency. A *dying* person, yes. Besides, Red would just send me back home with that annoying supercilious attitude of his."

Miles asked sharply, "You *do* have your cane with you, don't you?"

"Of course I do! I only ditch it when I'm home," said Myrtle.

Amos's home was a stone house on a quiet street that backed up to the lake. He had a heavily landscaped yard with many different trees and bushes. Puddin's old sedan was parked out front along with Puddin. When she spotted Miles's car approaching, she jumped out and stumbled over to meet them before they'd managed to get out of the car.

"Dead! Dead!" Puddin hastily made the sign of the cross and then pointed a shaking finger at the stone house.

"Puddin, Southern Baptists don't cross themselves," said Myrtle. "And if the poor man is dead, he's hardly a threat. Why, you're white as a sheet!"

"He's a sneaky dead man!" growled Puddin.

Myrtle said, "I simply can't listen to any of this nonsense right now. I'm going in on the off-chance that Mr. Subers requires medical assistance."

"What's *she* doin' here?" Puddin's small eyes peered suspiciously at Wanda as the lanky psychic unfolded herself from the back seat of Miles's car.

"She's here for moral support and perhaps for information. She knew this situation would transpire before it did," said Myrtle as she strode toward the front door. Her cane thumped emphatically on the driveway as she walked.

"She's a witch," murmured Puddin, backing up as Wanda approached.

"Gifted," corrected Myrtle without turning around. "She's gifted."

Miles looked torn between monitoring the Puddin and Wanda situation and following Myrtle. "Do you need me inside, Myrtle?"

Myrtle turned around at the front door. "It's up to you." She carefully removed a tissue from her pocketbook and turned the front door handle.

Wanda said gruffly to Puddin, "I been tryin' to tell you, yer in danger."

Puddin yelped, put her hands over her ears, and backed farther away.

"Coming," said Miles to Myrtle and speedily joined her as they went inside.

The house was well-lit with lots of large windows. Miles said, "Are you sure that the tissue was necessary? As far as we know, Amos's death was natural."

"Do you trust Puddin to be explicit with the details? She's not exactly the most reliable witness," said Myrtle. She glanced around the home. "I didn't realize that Amos was still such a reader."

There were books lining most of the walls—both in bookcases and in stacks. Amos had apparently skipped any official cataloging of these books, as they were shoved in the bookcases however they'd fit best.

Myrtle and Miles walked cautiously into the living room. There was a game show playing on the television set, which lent a spooky background noise to the home.

Myrtle sniffed. "There's clear evidence that Puddin was here, all right. The house is a disaster, and the television is on. I bet she thought that Amos wasn't even at home and she took advantage of the opportunity to watch TV."

Miles said, "She did say that he was a sneaky dead man. We should have asked her where he was ... um ... reposing."

Myrtle steeled herself, "All right, I'm heading into the bedroom." Miles followed at a distance as if reluctant to disturb the privacy of the dead man.

But there was no body there. There was simply an untidy bedroom with an old robe strewn across an unmade bed. Myrtle checked to make sure there wasn't a very thin Amos Subers under the robe (she hadn't seen him for a while). Seeing nothing, she walked back out to the living room.

"Perhaps Puddin was hallucinating," suggested Miles.

"Perhaps Puddin fell asleep during her game show and *dreamed* she saw Amos dead," said Myrtle, getting irritated. "Instead of looking for bodies, we could be back home playing Scrabble and eating pimento cheese sandwiches."

"Except that Red eliminated your bread supply," said Miles. "We still haven't checked Amos's kitchen."

"Yes, but we can see most of the kitchen from where we are and I don't see bodies littering the floor. I only see a kitchen that needs cleaning," said Myrtle.

Miles walked carefully into the kitchen as if dead bodies might pop out of the pantries at him. He walked around the island in the center of the kitchen and stopped short, grimacing. "I've found him. Completely concealed by the kitchen island."

"Sneaky indeed," said Myrtle breathlessly as she hurried over to where Miles stood. There was Amos. He was, most definitely, dead. A glass bottle lay on the floor beside him and he lay in a puddle of blood.

Miles cautiously checked for a pulse, just to make sure. He looked at Myrtle and shook his head. "I'm calling Red," he said firmly.

"Fine," said Myrtle in a distracted tone. "I wonder who on earth did this?"

Miles said as he dialed the phone number, "I'd imagine Puddin would be a likely suspect."

"Puddin?" said Myrtle in a scornful voice. "Puddin doesn't have the sense to murder anyone."

Miles said, "It's rather telling that the murder weapon appears to be a bottle of cleaning solution, isn't it? Almost as if the killer were making a final point of some sort."

Myrtle snorted. "Puddin is too foolish to make points. That glass bottle could be vinegar or olive oil or any number of things." She walked around the other side of the island and peered at the bottle from a distance. "All right. It appears to be a homemade cleaner. It looks like an old, glass vinegar bottle with a spray nozzle attached to the top. That thing was probably heavy as lead. Remember, Puddin didn't like his homemade cleaning stuff because she said it was stinky. Even if it was homemade cleaning solution, Puddin brought *my* cleaning products in here. In fact, I need to track those down."

Their conversation stopped for a few minutes while Miles spoke with Red on the phone, giving him a quick summary.

"He'll be right over," he said and then stopped short with a frown at the sound of a siren.

"Small towns," said Myrtle with a shrug. "He's never very far away."

Myrtle walked around curiously. She spotted a desk in the living room and used her tissue to lift things off of Amos's desk and peer at them.

"Anything interesting?" asked Miles. He walked over to the window and glanced outside.

"Not particularly. He really could have used a filing system. Oh wait, here's his desk calendar," said Myrtle.

The siren grew closer. Miles said, still looking out the window, "It looks as if progress is happening outside. Puddin appears to be actually listening to Wanda."

Myrtle snorted. "Probably because Puddin is in shock. Those two women are like oil and water. Now let's see about this calendar." She pulled out her phone from her pocketbook and took a couple of pictures, carefully turning the pages with her tissue. "It looks as though Amos had a fairly active social life."

Miles said, "I did seem to see him out a lot."

"Did you? That's surprising, since *you're* not out a lot," said Myrtle in a distracted voice.

Miles said stiffly, "I meant when I was out running errands. *I'm* running errands and he's socializing."

"It's your own fault that you're not socializing. You know that every old lady in town has set her cap for you. You just *choose* to go to the post office and the drugstore instead of going out to eat," said Myrtle.

Miles said, "I like to take things slow, that's all." He frowned at Myrtle.

"That's something we can agree on. Now, more about Amos's socializing. With whom was he doing it?" She turned another page of the desk calendar. "Perhaps Philomena Fant?"

Miles said, "That must be a very helpful calendar. Yes, I've seen him walking into Bo's Diner with Philomena."

"How about Alice Porper?" asked Myrtle. She made a face as the sound of the siren came right in front of the house. "Pooh. I'll have to wrap this up. And I didn't even find a cell phone."

"I *usually* saw him with Alice. But lately it's been Philomena with him. I remember thinking to myself that he might be two-timing Alice," said Miles.

Myrtle raised her eyebrows as she stepped away from the desk. "Is that because Amos appeared to be friendly with Philomena?"

"Very friendly indeed," said Miles.

"Interesting. I suppose he was a handsome man with those dark eyes and that lean build. And I seem to remember a particularly engaging smile. I never could get around that beard, though," said Myrtle. "It could be quite full on occasion."

A voice behind them said, "Please tell me that Amos Subers had a natural death."

They turned to see Red coming through the door.

"Afraid not," said Myrtle. "Looks as though he was conked on the head by a glass bottle." She paused. "It *probably* has cleaning solution in it. Puddin mentioned that he had homemade cleaners and he was certainly cheap enough to use them."

Red groaned. "Investigating murder was not on my list of things to do today."

Myrtle said, "Does this mean that I need to do my own grocery shopping? Because I don't really have food in my house now."

Red said to Miles, "Can you drive her to the store?"

Miles nodded.

"Okay, where's Amos? And then, if you two could be so kind as to step outside and join Puddin and Wanda? I'll talk to you out there after I've called the state police. I want our conversation to be private, too—I wanted to ask you about Puddin," said Red.

They pointed to the kitchen island and then headed for the door. As they walked outside, Myrtle muttered to Miles, "I simply can't allow Puddin to be arrested for murder. My house will be even more of a wreck than it is now."

"You always complain about what a terrible housekeeper she is. Maybe this is the opportunity to find someone new," said Miles as they walked toward Puddin and Wanda.

"*Wanting* someone new and *finding* someone new are two different things. This town only has so many cleaning ladies and they're always booked. What's more, I can't *afford* anyone better than Puddin. I can barely afford Puddin! No, I need to clear Puddin's name and make sure that I track down who's responsible for this. And, if Amos really was dating two women at once, I know where to start," said Myrtle.

Puddin, who had been gazing at Wanda with a rather awed expression, hurried toward them when she spotted them. "He were dead, weren't he? Deader than a doornail!"

Myrtle said, "Yes, Amos Subers is unfortunately deceased."

Puddin pointed at Wanda. "She knows about it, too!"

Myrtle said sharply, "Wanda knows about lots of things she has no involvement with. What I'm interested in is your *own* involvement with this issue."

Puddin looked sullen. "Ain't got nuthin' to do with it. Him just died."

"No, him *didn't* just die. He was eased along the way. First off, where are my cleaning bottles?"

Red suddenly snorted behind them. "Trust you to ask the important questions first, Mama."

"Well, Puddin took them from my house with every intent of using them. I'm curious to know where they are since I looked through Amos's house and didn't see them," said Myrtle.

Puddin, mindful of the officer of the law nearby, said with a nervous laugh, "Just borrowed 'em. They're in my car." She nodded to the old sedan.

Red said, "As much as I'm glad that y'all have determined the location of Mama's precious cleaning bottles, I'm going to need to talk to you alone, Puddin."

Puddin's already pasty-white face turned whiter, and she started howling. "Don't wanna go to jail!"

Red rolled his eyes to the heavens as if searching for some patience in the clouds. Apparently having found some, he gently said to Puddin, "I didn't say I was arresting you, merely asking you a few questions. You're vital to this investigation, having been the first person on the scene. I need to hear all about it."

Puddin looked drawn between panic and pride at being someone who knew something. She nodded reluctantly and Red took out his notebook and pen. They walked over to Red's police cruiser so that Puddin could sit while Red took notes.

Wanda gazed silently at the tableau. Myrtle figured that she'd probably never seen so much crying in her lifetime.

Myrtle said, "Do you have any ideas about this, Wanda? You knew Puddin was in danger ... is that because she was here right after the murderer was, or because she's in danger of going to prison?"

Wanda said, "The sight don't work that way."

Miles, never a fan of the sight, gave a gusty sigh.

Wanda continued, "I done talked to her. Puddin. She's gonna tell you everythin' she knows. Wants you to help figure it all out. I gots to go."

"Go?" asked Miles in alarm. "You can't walk all the way back home, Wanda. And I can't drive you there right now, either."

"Goin' to walk to the diner for some food," said Wanda. She held out her hand to display a leathery handful of quarters.

Miles reached in his pocket and pulled out his wallet. He carefully counted out a few bills and thrust them at Wanda. "In case you want more."

She smiled at him and loped off.

Miles muttered, "I'm surprised she's still hungry after eating at your place."

"Wanda is *always* hungry. Besides, it wasn't exactly a feast at my house, not after Red ate most of the sandwich stuff," said Myrtle.

Miles glanced back over at Puddin and Red and said, "You don't think Red believes Puddin had anything to do with this?"

Chapter Four

"**R**ed likes a case closed by the simplest means possible. But no, I'm sure in his heart of hearts that he doesn't think Puddin is a killer. Puddin is obnoxious, lazy, and foolish, but she's no murderer. And I really do need to keep my domestic help situation stable," said Myrtle, a fervent tone in her voice.

Miles said with a frown, "The thing that bothers me is that she didn't bring your cleaning products inside. They're still in the car. She couldn't exactly have forgotten them, considering that the entire reason she was at Amos's house was to clean it."

"But this is Puddin we're talking about. Maybe she knew that he had cleaning products in his house already. Perhaps she wanted them because the *next* house she was going to needed all-purpose cleaner or glass cleaner or what-have-you. Or maybe even the house she was going to *tomorrow* didn't have cleaning products inside. Puddin likely thought it was a more effective argument to tell me that the very next house she was cleaning didn't have them," said Myrtle.

Miles's face was doubtful. "I suppose so."

Myrtle said, "Think about the situation, Miles. Puddin was mad. She doesn't like cleaning in the first place, and then sud-

34

denly she's thrust into a situation where she is not even being *paid* for her work. This makes her furious."

Miles added dryly, "Furious enough to hit Amos over the head with a glass bottle? Furious is probably not the word we want to use around Red if we want to keep Puddin from being arrested."

"Point taken. So Puddin is *concerned* that she hasn't been paid. However, being a conscientious employee, she shows up for her designated cleaning day anyway," said Myrtle. She plopped down on a handy garden bench and made room as Miles sat down beside her.

Miles said, "That's laying it on thick, don't you think? Red is actually acquainted with Puddin. In fact, he's known her for a number of years. She's never conscientious. She probably went to Amos's house today with no intention of cleaning at all. She didn't even bring the cleaning bottles in. She went over there for the sole purpose of demanding her money."

"Money he *owed* her," corrected Myrtle with a frown. "You're making her sound like someone who was working for a mob boss instead of an employee cheated out of her pay. But I'll agree with you—mostly because Puddin shows up at even my house determined to clean as little as possible. She walks inside and doesn't see Amos. She decides, as Puddin would, to watch brain-numbing television in the form of a game show. Then she likely wants to fix herself something to drink or eat because ... it's Puddin. She believes that your refrigerator is her refrigerator. She sees Amos, freaks out, and calls us."

Miles said, "We can see if our theory is right in a few minutes. Looks like Red has finished with her and is heading over to us."

Red was indeed heading their way, and he looked grim. Puddin remained in the back of the police car, an obstinate expression on her face. The state police pulled up and Red spoke with them for a few minutes before turning back to Myrtle and Miles.

Myrtle said, "You seem upset, Red."

"Upset? Can't imagine what I have to be upset by." Red enumerated the issues on his fingers as he went. "My stomach is complaining about the alfalfa or whatever the abomination was I ate this morning before I ended up at your house. My mother has a habit of finding bodies."

Myrtle pursed her lips in displeasure. "I didn't find this one. You haven't been paying attention."

"I have a murder to investigate. What's more, I may need to find a new housekeeper for my aforementioned elderly mother because her current one is under suspicion of murder.

Miles looked concerned. "You suspect Puddin?"

"How can I *not* suspect Puddin? Puddin incriminated herself all over the place when I was talking with her. She has no filter whatsoever," said Red. "And I know that it was Amos who was Puddin's issue earlier. Remember our conversation at your house, Mama? You said Puddin was worse than usual because someone owed her money. I'd say that was a pretty good motive, wouldn't you?"

"I'd say it was a good motive if it was anyone but Puddin. Surely you can't imagine that Puddin could murder someone!

Puddin is a lot of things, but she's never done anything illegal," said Myrtle hotly.

Red said, "She's been sneaky, though."

"But sneaky and dishonest are two different things. Puddin might not show up for work and she might prevaricate and say that her back is thrown and she can't clean. She might even walk out with my cleaning supplies." Myrtle stopped and frowned. She'd lost track of where she was going with that.

"Yes?" asked Red.

It came back to her and she said, "But she's never taken any of my things before."

"Besides your cleaning supplies, you mean," said Red, rolling his eyes.

"Exactly. Which don't count because she parades out the front door with them. I swear, she's more like a sullen child. She doesn't go around murdering people, even if they owe her money," said Myrtle.

"Okay. Settle down, Mama. I don't have time to drive you over to the doctor to get your blood pressure checked out. We're finished with Puddin for right now. Why don't you and Miles take her home? Dusty can bring her back later to pick up her car. She needs to wind down a little," said Red. He glanced around. "And where's Wanda?"

"Gone to eat again. We'll drive her home when she's back."

"Guess you'll have a full carload," said Red to Miles with a chuckle.

Miles nodded glumly.

A sedan pulled up and a tall, muscular man with a very short haircut stepped out. "Lieutenant Perkins!" drawled Myrtle as he approached them. "What a delight. You know I always look forward to seeing you again."

"Even though that means yet another homicide victim in the town of Bradley," muttered Red.

Perkins smiled at Myrtle, which pleased her more than a handshake or hug would do. That's because Perkins was usually stony-faced and stern. "It's a pleasure to see you again, Mrs. Clover, despite the circumstances. And hello to you, too, Mr. Bradford. Mrs. Clover, I'd love to hear your opinion on what you've seen so far here."

Myrtle beamed at him and Red put a hand up to his temple as if it were pounding. He never liked the fact that Perkins put great stock into Myrtle's insights. But in Myrtle's eyes, this trait of Perkins made him a most capable detective.

Myrtle gave him a short rundown of the day. Finishing up, she said, shooting a sideways glance at Red, "Although it may, to the *unimaginative eye*, appear that my cleaning woman, Puddin, had something to do with this murder, I can assure you that she did not." Red muttered something unintelligible under his breath.

Perkins nodded and put away his notebook, looking at Myrtle thoughtfully. "It sounds as though you have a lot of affection for Puddin."

Miles snorted in disbelief, causing Myrtle to shoot him a quelling look.

Myrtle said, "Ordinarily, Puddin is the bane of my existence. But yes, I can't help but feel a certain fondness for her. At any rate, I know what Puddin is and isn't. She's no killer."

"Did you know Amos Subers at all?" asked Perkins.

"Know him? Well, I taught him," said Myrtle.

Miles raised his eyebrows in surprise and Myrtle frowned at him, "None of that, Miles. Amos is in his early sixties. I was a mere child when I taught him."

This time Red snorted and Myrtle hissed, "There seems to be a horrible cold virus among us."

Perkins said mildly, "What sort of impression did you have of Mr. Subers? As a teacher or otherwise?"

Myrtle considered this. "He was bookish, but he didn't care a thing about his grades. He was very lackadaisical about turning in homework. One thing I always noticed was that he was distracting in the classroom."

Perkins asked, "Distracting in what way?"

"The girls always knocked themselves out to get his attention. They were quite energetic in their efforts. But he'd keep his nose in his books. He was a nice-looking boy, but it occurred to me at the time that a good part of his appeal was how he appeared ... distant. Removed. Disinterested," said Myrtle.

Red said, "I'll point out that these observations were from forty years ago. Let's allow that the poor guy might have changed in his lifetime."

Miles cleared his throat. "Actually, I can verify that Amos Subers is still considered something of a catch. He's apparently quite the ladies' man. Although I don't have a theory on his appeal."

Myrtle said, "Judging from the books in his home, maybe his allure is the same thing—an aloofness."

Perkins nodded, taking it all in for a few moments. Then he said, "Thanks for this. And I'm sure I'll see you later." He and

Red walked toward the house slowly, with Red filling him in on the details of the case as they went.

Myrtle motioned to Puddin to get out of the open door of the police car and walk over. Puddin heaved herself out of the cruiser and slouched over to them. "So hungry," she said grouchily.

"Hunger is the least of your worries," said Myrtle sternly. "Pull yourself together. What kind of foolishness have you been spouting to Red? He seems to think it's a possibility you're somehow involved in this mess."

Puddin started howling like a toddler. Myrtle snapped, "Stop that! I'm already miffed with you, Puddin. You've put me in the position of saying nice things about you for the last hour."

Puddin gave a shuddering sigh and prodigious sniff. Myrtle rummaged in her tremendous purse for a packet of tissues, which she thrust impatiently at Puddin.

"Now, what happened?" asked Myrtle.

Puddin said, "Went in to clean and old Amos was dead."

"Yes, I've grasped that part of the narrative. Now tell me the *rest* of what happened."

"The door was unlocked, but he weren't particular about that. Walked in and shouted for Mr. Subers."

"*Shouted* for him?" asked Miles.

"Owed me money!" said Puddin, glowering.

"And did you report that detail to Red? The shouting and the owing of money and whatnot?" asked Myrtle.

Puddin gave a hesitant nod as if sensing that this was perhaps not the best tack to have taken.

Myrtle pursed her lips.

Puddin said in a defensive voice, "Mama told me not to lie!"

"She probably also told you if you didn't have something nice to say, not to say anything at all," said Myrtle. "And telling Red that Mr. Subers was a tightwad was probably not the way to go."

Puddin was suddenly struck with a thought. "Now he's dead and I can't get my money!"

"His beneficiaries might be inclined to settle his debts," said Myrtle.

Puddin squinted suspiciously at her again.

Myrtle said, "Go on with the story. I'm assuming there was no answer when you shouted for Mr. Subers."

"Figured he was avoiding me," Puddin said in a sullen voice. "So I sat down to relax."

"Because you were so worn out," said Myrtle, rolling her eyes.

"From cleanin' your house!" said Puddin.

"My house isn't clean enough for you to be exhausted," said Myrtle.

Miles smiled.

"Well, I didn't sleep good last night," Puddin snarled. "Anyway, game shows was on. I settled down to watch. Then I wanted a little somethin' to snack on." Her eyes were shifty.

"I've no doubt," said Myrtle. "This all sounds very familiar."

"So I went into the kitchen to look in his pantry. An' there he was!" Puddin threw up her hands to indicate the impertinence of the dead man.

"And then you called us in complete hysteria," said Myrtle.

"Didn't think Dusty was home," said Puddin. Her stomach growled loudly, and she sighed at its emptiness.

Myrtle squinted down the street. "The cavalry is coming."

Miles looked too. "In a most unlikely guise."

Puddin frowned suspiciously and watched as Wanda approached them. Now that she was closer, they could see that she was clutching a white bag.

"I do believe that's a takeout bag from Bo's Diner," said Myrtle.

Miles said, "Which is easy enough to guess, considering that the bag is dripping grease."

Puddin didn't seem to mind the grease one bit. She grabbed the bag when Wanda proffered it and hastily dug into the fries and hot dog, giving Wanda a grateful smile.

"Figured you was hungry," said Wanda, carefully picking her words so as not to include any mention of prophecy.

Puddin managed a smile as she quickly consumed the contents of the bag.

Miles said, "All right, I suppose I should start the process of getting everyone back home. I know how to get Wanda back home, but I'm not exactly sure where you live, Puddin."

Puddin said, "I got my car here."

Miles said, "Yes, but Red didn't want you driving, considering how upset you've been."

Myrtle said, "We should take Puddin home first, unless Wanda has plans."

Wanda arched her brows as if to say that plans were not usually a major part of her life.

"All right, Puddin's house it is. Besides, I need to talk to Dusty for a few minutes," said Myrtle.

They climbed into Miles's car after getting Myrtle's cleaning products out of Puddin's vehicle. Miles winced at Puddin's greasy bag but didn't say a word as she continued eating.

Chapter Five

Puddin's house was a crooked little place plopped on a large lot that made the house look even smaller than it was. The yard was a riot of weeds and knee-high grass and the home was ringed by dead bushes. Considering that Dusty was a yardman by trade, it recalled the old saying, "the shoemaker's children go barefoot."

Puddin leaned forward in the car to peer at the driveway. "He's home," she said with a shrug.

"Excellent," said Myrtle as Miles parked the car.

Wanda pushed open the car door on her side, but shook her head when Myrtle gestured for her to come along. "I'll sit here. Got some visions comin' through."

Puddin looked alarmed and hurried away from the car as if the incoming visions might explode like bombs around her. Belatedly remembering her manners, she mumbled a thanks to Wanda for her lunch.

Dusty, although home, did not look pleased to see them. In fact, he looked aghast as Puddin again burst into tears at the sight of him. He gave her an awkward pat on the back. "Somethin' happen?" he asked as he gestured for them to come in. He spotted Wanda sitting in Miles's car and stared curiously at her but didn't say a thing.

The interior of the home attested to Puddin's general lack of interest in housekeeping. While somewhat clean, there was clutter on every available surface of the home.

Myrtle said, "Puddin happened upon a body today."

Dusty stared at her. "At yer house?"

"All the bodies in this town aren't found at my house, you know. This one belonged to Amos Subers," said Myrtle.

Dusty nodded. "Puddin cleans there but I don't do his yard."

"I figured as much," said Myrtle. The yard had actually appeared fairly well-kept.

Puddin stemmed the flow of tears long enough to holler, "They think I did it, Dusty, because he owed me money! But I didn't. He was all right. I sorta liked him, actually." Here Puddin looked a bit cagey. She had apparently reached the conclusion that it would be better for her to profess admiration for the dead man instead of playing up his indebtedness to her.

"What did you like about him?" asked Myrtle in a pressing manner.

"The house weren't never that messy, so cleanin' was easy. Not like yours," said Puddin cuttingly.

"What I'm curious about," said Myrtle, "is what you were doing between the time you left my house and the time you went to Amos Subers' house."

Puddin frowned. "I went right to his house." She glanced at Miles who appeared fascinated with the amount of clutter in the housekeeper's house. "Have a seat," she said.

"There's no way you did. I simply don't believe you spent that much time watching game shows at his house," said Myrtle.

Miles, who didn't seem to want to rebuff Puddin's offer of hospitality, glanced desperately around for a suitable surface for him to park his rear on.

Puddin quickly said, "Oh. I went and ate."

Miles eyed the greasy bag that she was still clutching in a chubby hand.

Myrtle drawled, "Try again, Puddin. Third time's the charm."

Puddin drew in a deep breath. "I were with Dusty."

Dusty blinked at her. "At whut time?" He'd been watching Miles's increasingly desperate attempts to find a seat. Dusty walked to a chair and unceremoniously upended it, allowing all the assorted wrappers, unopened mail, and catalogs to fall to the floor. He motioned to Miles to have a seat which Miles gingerly did. Myrtle shook her head impatiently when Dusty offered to create a place for her to sit.

"I was with you this mornin'," she snapped. "You remember." It was more of a command than a question.

"I remember wakin' *up* an' you was there," said Dusty. He did not seem to be onboard with being an alibi.

"You're confused about the time," insisted Puddin. "We never put much stock in clocks." She nodded at a wall clock that displayed a time that might have been correct on the west coast.

"If you say I *wasn't* with you this mornin'," Puddin said in a voice that was both helpful reminder as well as a threat, "then they thinks I killed him."

Dusty gave this a moment's thought before he said gruffly, "Ah. That musta been when you got me breakfast."

"Breakfast. Yes," said Puddin in relief.

"A breakfast which Puddin clearly didn't partake in," said Myrtle with a sigh. "Never mind. We'll eventually get to the bottom of it all. Puddin, since you spent a good deal of time in Amos's house, perhaps you can help us determine who might have wanted to kill him."

Puddin looked at her television set as though she wanted to have nothing to do with any further discussion of Amos Subers, alive or dead.

Miles said, "If we had another suspect besides you, it would help."

Put this way, Puddin looked thoughtful. "He had a black eye not long ago. It's gone now."

"Who hit him?" asked Myrtle.

"Him was datin' that smarty-pants woman. Philomena. From the library," said Puddin, squinting up her face in her effort to produce thoughts.

Myrtle raised her eyebrows. "A librarian gave him a black eye? That somehow seems out of character."

Puddin shook her head. "Nope. Her brother gave it to him."

"Who told you that?" asked Myrtle. Puddin sometimes wasn't the most reliable source of information.

Puddin said indignantly, "Him himself! I asked why his eye was black and he told me. Simple as that. I see the brother around and about. He dates a waitress at Bo's Diner." Her eyes gleamed with gossipy glee.

"Did he elaborate as to *why* Philomena-the-librarian's brother happened to give him a black eye? Because it all sounds rather extraordinary," said Myrtle.

Puddin shook her head again. "Nope. But I asked Bitty."

Bitty was one of Puddin's many cousins and an accomplished gossip. She was, also, decidedly not bitty, but rather rotund.

Myrtle felt as though she were pulling teeth. "And Bitty said what?"

"That her brother hit him because of his sister," said Puddin.

Myrtle said, "Okay. One other question—did you see or hear anything when you arrived at Amos Subers' house?"

Puddin squinted in deep thought. "That awful dog next door was barking at me. I barked back."

Myrtle sighed. "I mean, anything that might have a bearing at all on Amos's murder."

Puddin resumed squinting. "Saw her leave."

"Saw *whom* leave?" asked Myrtle.

"That Alice. The other woman he was seeing," said Puddin. She looked longingly at the television set again and appeared to glance around for a remote. Miles, still perched on the chair, looked alarmed at the prospect of adding a blaring TV to the general chaos of the room.

Myrtle realized this was as much information as she was going to be able to get from Puddin, as dissatisfying as that was.

"Before we leave, Dusty, I need you to do something for me," said Myrtle.

Dusty looked at her in alarm. "Too hot to mow!" he howled.

"No, no. You mowed a couple of days ago, remember?" said Myrtle.

"Them gnomes," he said with a sigh.

"Yes, please," said Myrtle. "And if you could do it this afternoon, that would be ideal. I've found it's more effective when the gnomes are pulled out directly following an infraction by Red."

"What wuz it this time?" asked Dusty with idle curiosity.

"My cane," said Myrtle, grimacing.

Dusty glanced down at the offending object which Myrtle was clutching in her right hand. "Seems to me yer usin' it."

"Yes, but he wants me to use it in my own *home*. I know the way *perfectly* in my house and can touch various pieces of furniture if I need support. Plus, Red has been especially sassy lately. Anyway, can you make it?" asked Myrtle impatiently.

Dusty glanced at the nearby wall clock. "Yep."

"That clock is three hours behind," said Myrtle.

"Still works if you do math," said Dusty with dignity.

Miles and Myrtle joined Wanda in Miles's car. Miles set off for Wanda's house.

"Anything good in the vision department?" asked Myrtle.

In response, Wanda silently handed Myrtle a piece of paper on which she'd scrawled what looked like ancient hieroglyphics but what Myrtle knew was intended to be modern-day English.

"Ah. The weekly horoscope for Sloan, then?" asked Myrtle. She gave the slip of paper a look of trepidation. "And on the back of what appears to be one of Miles's gas receipts."

Wanda shrugged a thin shoulder. "The visions wuz comin' in. Had ter record them."

Myrtle nodded and carefully put the piece of paper into her pocketbook. "I'll transcribe this later and hand it in to Sloan." Sloan Jones was the editor of the *Bradley Bugle* newspaper where Wanda published a horoscope column. Myrtle had a helpful hints column there, but much preferred writing investigative reports for Sloan. And she had a good article for him today.

A good while later, Miles pulled up to Wanda's hubcap-covered house.

"Let us know if there are any developments," said Myrtle. "Or if anything interesting pops up on your radar." She glanced around at the unwelcoming red clay, the cars standing on cement blocks like mechanical statues on pedestals, and the large rocks scattered through the clay. "Where is this garden going?"

Wanda beamed at the mention of the garden. "Near the door. One of them pocket gardens."

Myrtle peered at the front door. There was an old cooler there that had 'live bayt!' written on it in what looked like paint. There was also a tire, a plastic bucket that was so old it was nearly white, an overflowing garbage can, and a crumpled tarp. She said, "I do love your sense of adventure, Wanda. And I'm sure that the garden club gala will likely have someone lecturing about pocket gardens there."

Wanda bestowed her with another gap-toothed smile and happily walked into her house.

Miles said as he drove off down the rural highway toward Bradley, "I'm not sure that Wanda will fit in very well with the rest of the garden club."

"Well, she fits in well with me. And *I* fit in well with garden club. If garden club knows what's good for them, they'll be charmed and delighted to have her there at the gala," said Myrtle with a sniff.

Miles's expression was doubtful.

"Where are we going now?" asked Miles. "To the grocery store? Considering that you now have less food than you had to begin with?"

"No time for groceries yet, Miles. We're hot on the trail," said Myrtle. "Let's run by the *Bugle* office so I can let Sloan know about my coverage of the Subers murder. Then we can visit Philomena at the library."

"Glad you're keeping your editor so updated," said Miles. "He doesn't mind that you assign yourself all the big stories?"

"Sloan is grateful for the help," said Myrtle, waving her hand dismissively. "It's a small-town newspaper without a lot of resources. He'll be absolutely delighted that I'm taking it on."

"Even though Red won't want you to have anything remotely to do with the story or the case itself?" asked Miles. "That doesn't sound like Sloan."

"Red wouldn't dare try to stop me. He'll already face my gnome army later in the day. He wouldn't want to try my patience again," said Myrtle in a confident tone.

Miles drove grimly on.

As Miles had predicted, Sloan's face did not exactly reflect the delight Myrtle had claimed it would. Instead, he looked anxious—as he usually did whenever his former English teacher stopped by the newsroom.

"Ah, Amos Subers. Yes." Bits of perspiration beaded up on the big man's face and neck. "Which reminds me! I had someone rave about your helpful hints column yesterday. He praised it up one side and down the other! Said that he'd tried out your suggestion about using a drying rack to keep his plastics still in the dishwasher and that it was a *life changer*!"

Myrtle frowned at him. "Why are you trying to change the subject, Sloan? I'm not here to talk about helpful hints. I don't get the same professional satisfaction in helping people prevent static cling as I do when writing an investigative article on crime in Bradley. Besides, they aren't *my* tips. They're reader tips that I share. I simply wanted to let you know that I'll work on the Subers story so that you wouldn't write the article yourself."

Sloan swallowed. His face was miserable. "It's just that Red stopped by here on the way over to the police station and asked me to keep you from getting involved in that piece."

Miles shook his head and started thumbing through some old copies of the *Bugle* on a nearby desk.

Myrtle sighed and looked at the ceiling as if patience might somehow be found there. It apparently wasn't because she looked back at Sloan and said, "This is how it works. You try to keep me from writing stories that Red doesn't want me to write. I push back. You fold. I write an amazing story that people are talking about for days. Can we go ahead and skip the argument? After all, it *is* a free press." She rummaged in her large pocketbook and removed a slip of paper, dangling it tantalizingly in front of Sloan's face. "Do you know what this is?"

Sloan squinted at it. "A gasoline receipt?"

"That is correct. It's a gasoline receipt as well as being a treasure trove of Wanda's latest predictions," said Myrtle. "Unfortunately, visions struck Wanda while she was sitting in the backseat of Miles's car. This is the result."

Miles gave an admiring chuckle. Wanda's column was a tremendous hit for the town of Bradley. Her predictions were alarmingly precise and direct, to the extent that the good citizens of Bradley held their collective breaths whenever a new one was published.

Sloan took the slip of paper, staring at it. "But this makes no sense at all, Miss Myrtle. I couldn't run this in the paper."

"Well, that's where I come in. By now, I'm an expert in deciphering Wanda's scribblings. As you know, I'm the one translating them. I just wanted to point out how much trouble you would be in if I *didn't* help you. Of course, if you *want* me to help you, you're tacitly acknowledging that I'm writing the Amos Subers story. Which only makes sense, considering I was one of the first people on the scene there," said Myrtle with a sniff.

Sloan slowly handed her back the paper. "You'll do a great job with the story," he said. He appeared to be relieved that their traditional push and pull over her assignments was over ... for the day, anyway.

Myrtle beamed at him. "Excellent. Now tell me how things are going with you. Are you and Sally Solomon still seeing each other?"

Sloan shook his head sadly. "I'm afraid we've hit a snag, Miss Myrtle. I've been so caught up with things at the paper that I believe I come across as sort of boring to her."

"Nonsense! I've known you for most of your life and I haven't found you boring at all," said Myrtle.

Miles cleared his throat. "What kinds of things are you talking about when you go out on dates?"

"Dates?" Sloan blinked at him.

Myrtle said, "Aren't the two of you going out for lunches or dinners or getting breakfast or seeing plays or concerts or anything?"

Sloan looked subdued. "Should we be? We usually either talk on the phone or else I drop by her house after work and we chat a little."

Myrtle said, "That's all wrong, Sloan. You should still be in the wining and dining phase. As Miles was asking, what types of things are you talking about when you're visiting each other?"

Sloan looked like a deer in the headlights. "You know. What stories I'm running in the next day's paper and how I'm redesigning the *Bugle* website. Stuff like that."

Miles winced.

Sloan said, "But she seems real interested in it. Sally even gave me some suggestions for the paper, like using more photos and having more of a visual approach to storytelling."

Myrtle said, "That's fine, but you need to branch out. You need to revisit topics like music, movies, books ... things like that." Her eyes grew wide, and she snapped her fingers. "I have a great idea! You should take her to the garden club gala. It will be an evening of food and plants."

Miles gave a muffled cough that sounded suspiciously like a laugh.

"The garden club gala," said Sloan slowly. "You know, I do think she likes plants. At least, I see them at her house."

Myrtle pulled out an envelope from her purse. "And, lucky for you, I'm selling tickets! Miles will be there, too."

Miles gave a gloomy nod of confirmation.

Sloan looked thoughtful. "Do you think that will help? Going to events and such?"

"It certainly won't hurt," said Myrtle.

Chapter Six

Afew minutes later, Myrtle and Miles got back in his car. "And I thought *I* was rusty at dating," said Miles as he drove off toward the library.

"You may be, but Sloan is a disaster," said Myrtle. "I don't have to be Wanda to see their relationship is doomed unless he makes changes. Think how helpful we were, Miles."

"He regaled his date with a discussion about revamping the newspaper website," marveled Miles.

"Which he's doing a *terrible* job at. He took the whole thing down to work on it and has been updating it in spurts. It looks as if the entire website is down," clucked Myrtle. She peered closer at Miles. "You look anxious, Miles. What's the trouble?"

Miles said, "I wish I'd known that we were going to the library today. I have an overdue book to return."

"Well, swing by your house first and pick it up. It isn't as if we live far away."

Miles shook his head. "I'm not done with the book yet." His face looked slightly green as it did whenever he contemplated doing anything remotely wrong.

Myrtle said, "I can tell you're wracked with guilt over this overdue book. What's the title?"

"It's the complete collection of Sherlock Holmes," said Miles. It appeared to grieve him to even mention the book.

"For heaven's sake, Miles, that's hardly a bestseller. I don't think that the town of Bradley is on pins and needles waiting for the book to be returned to the library. Just renew it."

Miles pulled into a parking place at the library. "I've already renewed it," he said miserably.

"Then renew it again! You're allowed two."

Miles unlocked their doors. "I've already renewed it twice. I'm reading it slowly and savoring every word. I thought we could apply some of Sherlock's methods to our investigations."

Myrtle got out of the car. "You mean we should have noted that Amos had a fierce argument with Philomena because of the evidence of a hastily tossed-aside library book and the carpet fibers on his shoes?"

Miles's eyes grew wide. "Did you notice that?"

"Don't be silly. Amos didn't even have shoes on. We'll have to be a lot sharper than that if we even try to be more like Sherlock." Myrtle gave Miles a narrowed look. "And don't feel the need to confess your overdue book to Philomena. It's not as if you owe the library much money."

"Fifty cents," said Miles, glumly.

"Just zip it, then. I want to focus her on Amos and their relationship and not have her thinking about missing books and fines and whatnot." Myrtle pushed open the library door.

"It's not *missing*," said Miles stiffly. "I know exactly where it is."

"Never mind that. Let's figure out which one is Philomena. I know I taught a Philomena Fant, but it was a million years ago. I do remember that she was a brilliant student, although her parents seemed to spoil her to pieces. They both came into the school and argued with me about giving Philomena an A-minus. Anyway, I'm quite sure her appearance has changed in the meantime. The library staff should wear nametags," said Myrtle irritably.

Miles seemed to be caught up in the spirit of Sherlock. "Let's use the process of elimination. From what I've heard about Amos's proclivities, I don't believe he was likely dating any of the male librarians."

Myrtle scanned the area. "True. And I don't see him dating that young woman over there. He seemed to date peers or near-peers."

"We should talk to the woman over there, then," said Miles, a triumphant note in his voice. He pointed to a dainty woman in her fifties with blonde hair hanging neatly around her face.

Myrtle nodded. "She seems a likely candidate. What's more, she resembles Alice Porper quite a bit. It looks as if Amos had a 'type.'"

They walked over to where Philomena was shelving books off a cart. She smiled at them as they approached, revealing dimples. "May I help you?" she asked. She had china-blue eyes, putting Myrtle in mind of her grandmother's Wedgewood. "And it's good to see you again, Miss Myrtle. I always enjoyed your English class."

Myrtle paused. She realized that this woman had taken part in some sort of a relationship with Amos and likely didn't even know that he had passed away. Here she was at work when she might have taken the afternoon off after such a revelation. Red must not have spoken to her yet. She decided it would be best to ease into questions. The last thing she wanted was an explosion of tears.

She cleared her throat. "It's good to see you too, Philomena. I remember your being an excellent student. And yes, you could give us a hand. Miles here has recently developed an interest in Sherlock Holmes. I thought there must be some sort of companion book he could read for additional information on the stories or maybe on the life of Doyle."

Miles blinked slowly at her.

Philomena said, "How interesting! Yes, I know I've seen such a book. Let me check in with the catalog on that computer over there."

As soon as Philomena had stepped away, Miles hissed at Myrtle, "I didn't really want to draw attention to me or my overdue Sherlock."

"Don't be silly. You'll enjoy the book and I needed to start a conversation that didn't immediately involve the murder of someone close to Philomena," said Myrtle.

They both stopped whispering and gave rather fake smiles as Philomena approached them again. She said, "If you'll follow me for a minute, I know just where we can find the book."

And she did. "This looks like the perfect companion read, Miles," said Myrtle, flipping through the pages. "It covers all things Sherlock." She looked at Philomena and said as an aside, "He's become quite obsessed with Sherlock and Watson."

Philomena's dimples were in attendance again. "Are you two planning on doing some investigating yourselves?" she asked.

Myrtle said, "Funny you should ask that. We certainly are. A trip to the library was in order after our rather disturbing morning. You see, we discovered the death this morning of someone in town. Amos Subers."

Philomena's eyes grew wide and she stepped back until the bookshelf partially supported her. "No," she whispered.

Miles didn't look enthused by the prospect of Philomena passing out on the floor, despite her tiny stature. He said gruffly, "Here, come and sit down."

Philomena allowed herself to be led to a study table and sat down quickly in a chair. "Are you sure?" she pressed them. "I saw him yesterday."

Myrtle said, "Oh dear. We didn't mean to upset you. You clearly must have known him. Unfortunately, yes, we're sure that he's passed away. And that he was murdered."

Philomena gave a big, shuddering sigh. Myrtle watched warily for the sign of tears.

"Yes, I knew him. How awful. We ... well, we used to be in a relationship." She looked at Myrtle through narrowed eyes. "You said it was *murder*?"

"I'm afraid so. There's no way he died from natural causes. But no worries, I'm sure that we'll—I mean, the police will—discover who was responsible and bring them to justice. Obviously, you hadn't heard anything about this yet," said Myrtle. "I'm sorry to be the bearer of bad news."

Philomena slowly shook her head. "I've been here working all morning." She said in a careful voice, "And I mean *all* morning. I've been busy shelving and checking out books and recording new acquisitions and helping with a research request. I had no idea that Amos was dead."

Miles said, "It's only been in the last few hours that he was. There was no way for you to know."

Myrtle said, "I was wondering what your impression of Amos was. What kind of person was he? I taught him ages ago and my impressions of him are a little skewed."

This made Philomena smile. "I can only imagine what impression he left on you as a student. Spitballs? Pencil fights? He was a few years older than me, so we weren't in school at the same time."

Myrtle raised her eyebrows. "Not at all, actually, but it's interesting that you would think he *would* have been that kind of a student. He was actually fairly academic and bookish. But he didn't care a whit about what his grades were."

Philomena nodded her head. "That makes sense. I was trying to imagine a *normal* teenaged boy, but Amos was anything but normal. That's one of the things that he and I had most in common—books. We shared a love of literature."

Miles said, "You should speak to our book club."

Myrtle and Miles were always looking for ways to improve the book club selections. They'd try foisting classic literature on the group but they would always return to beach reads.

Myrtle said, "Miles, what a brilliant idea! You're absolutely right. Philomena would be the perfect speaker. Then maybe she could recommend books for our club to take on."

Philomena's face was doubtful. "I don't know that I'm much of a speaker. Actually, the idea sort of terrifies me."

"But we can pay you!" said Myrtle. "Tippy has been collecting club dues for the past hundred years and all we ever spend it on is a rather anemic brunch at the end of the year. And you'll be able to push past your nervousness with your passion for books."

Miles said, "It sure would be nice to read Faulkner or Hemingway for a change."

"It's settled!" said Myrtle, beaming. She took a small notebook and a pen out of her pocketbook and jotted something down. "Here's Tippy's number. We have a meeting on Friday, actually."

Philomena paled. "That seems very soon."

"Yes, but it will be a nice distraction from poor Amos, won't it? And I promise you that our group is *anything* but scary," said Myrtle.

"Except for Erma Sherman," said Miles.

"Yes, but Erma is allergic to good literature. She likely won't even attend," said Myrtle. "But, goodness, I got so distracted that I forgot that you never really answered my question, my dear. Amos? What was he like? You mentioned that you both shared a love of books and then we got off-track."

Philomena said slowly, "He was ... rather wonderful, really. And *not*, all at the same time. He could be a profound thinker and share all of these marvelous ideas about the universe and life. But then he would be honed in on the here and now and wouldn't want to spend a couple of dollars for a sweet tea at the restaurant. He had this way of focusing on you as if you were the only person in the world ... until he didn't." Her voice was bitter.

Myrtle waited for a moment to see if any other remembrances were forthcoming. When they apparently weren't, she said, "Who could have done such a thing? It was clear that Amos must have had enemies. Not only was he murdered, but it was obvious that he'd been in some sort of a recent fight."

Philomena flushed. "The two things are likely unconnected. But I can tell you one person that he didn't get along with well. In fact, they had a public argument right here in the library."

Myrtle perked up. This sounded promising. "Who was it?"

"I don't know the woman's name, but I've seen her around town. She's short and has a dumpy physique. Lank blonde hair and a rather doughy complexion. She was yelling at him here ... something about money," said Philomena. "Amos waved her away as if she were some sort of annoying gnat."

Myrtle now seemed in a hurry to wrap up their conversation. "Well, thanks for this. It doesn't sound promising, though, does it? Even Amos didn't think it was important, considering he was waving her away."

Philomena said, "Really? Someone demanding money right before a murder doesn't seem important?"

"Not when it's a person like that. But you've been incredibly helpful with the Sherlock Holmes book," said Myrtle.

"Well, let me check it out for you," she said smoothly, heading for the circulation desk.

Miles's eyes widened behind his glasses. He whispered, "Myrtle! I can't have this book checked out on my card. She'll see my overdue book."

Myrtle said, "Pooh! No one cares about your fifty cents or whatever the meager fine is, Miles. It's hardly a moral failing to have a late library book." She stared at him. "You're perspiring profusely. Settle down."

Miles gave her a miserable look. "I don't want her to see that I'm overdue."

"For heaven's sake. I'll put it on my card and then you can return it with the other one or when you're ready." Myrtle fished out her library card. "It's not worth the agony."

Myrtle presented her library card to Philomena, who took it with a smile and another flash of her dimples.

"I hope you'll both enjoy the book. If you like it, I can find other, similar books. There's an excellent biography of Doyle that we have and then there are some interesting new Sherlock stories that you might enjoy," said Philomena.

"*New* stories?" asked Miles. "As in long-lost stories that Doyle wrote?"

"Oh no. No, these are written in the twenty-first century." Philomena handed Myrtle's card back to her.

Miles made a face. "I'm not sure I'd like those. I'm a stickler for reading the genuine article."

"But the Arthur Conan Doyle estate authorized these," said Philomena with a smile. "You might want to give them a try."

Myrtle and Miles walked out of the library with thoughtful expressions.

Myrtle said, "How about that?"

Miles said, "I know. Who'd have thought there could be *new* Sherlock Holmes stories?"

Myrtle shot him an impatient look. "I was talking about what Philomena was telling us."

"So was I." Miles unlocked his car with his key fob.

Myrtle said, "My stomach is entirely too empty to put up with your nonsense, Miles. First your unmerited fretfulness over your library book. And now you're obsessed with Sherlock again. We're supposed to be reading *1984* for book club."

Miles shrugged. "I've read *1984* quite a few times over the years. I could probably give a lecture on the book. And you, as I recall your saying, taught the thing for at least twenty years. So it's the last book we should read right now."

They climbed into the car. Miles took the Sherlock book from Myrtle and then reached into his center console. He pulled out a travel container of disinfecting wipes and carefully wiped down the plastic library book cover.

Myrtle raised her eyebrows as she watched him. "I had no idea your OCD behavior extended quite this far, Miles."

He didn't even look up as he finished the front and spine of the book and moved on to the back cover. "You can't be too careful. Who knows how many hands have handled this book?"

"Not very many, from the looks of it. It appears to be practically new and yet it must be decades old," said Myrtle.

"Now it's decades old and disinfected," said Miles with satisfaction. He removed another wipe and wiped down his own hands before slowly backing out of the parking space.

"We're heading toward the grocery store, I suppose?" asked Miles.

Myrtle made a face. "I don't think I'm ready to face the crowd at the store, especially at lunchtime. Besides, I don't even have a list. If I go to the store hungry without a list, I'm sure to blow my budget to smithereens. Let's go to Bo's Diner. I have a real hankering for a 99-cent pimento cheese dog and chili fries. Now *that's* budget-friendly."

"That makes my stomach hurt, thinking about it," said Miles as he drove quickly to the diner.

"You can always get the veggie plate," said Myrtle with a shrug.

"It's just as bad. Everything is fried," said Miles.

"How else are you supposed to eat okra?" demanded Myrtle.

Chapter Seven

Miles pulled up to the diner moments later. Bo's Diner had been a fixture in Bradley for at least forty years. The current owner was the original Bo's grandson, since his father had recently retired from the job, and despite his youth, didn't apparently dare to make any changes for fear of being haunted by the ghost of his grandfather. The floors were ancient linoleum, the high-backed vinyl booths faced Formica-topped tables, and the walls were dark laminate wood paneling. The decorations in the diner consisted of signs with sayings like 'The language you use in church is good enough to use in here.'

Their waitress, Pam, grinned at them and told them they could sit anywhere. Myrtle was glad that she didn't call her *sugar*. There were waitresses in Bo's Diner who were under the mistaken impression that Myrtle was six years old. Pam, fortunately, was not one of them.

Myrtle plopped down in an ancient booth and didn't even glance at the laminated menu. "I already know what I want."

Miles carefully studied the menu, both the front and the back. "I wish they would serve breakfast all day. I'm really more in the mood for breakfast."

"Ask them," said Myrtle with a shrug. "This isn't a white tablecloth dining experience. They'd probably be happy to give you an egg."

Pam came back with a grin. "I see that the menus are lying on the table. Y'all ready to order?"

Miles hesitated and Myrtle said impatiently, "He's too reluctant to cause any trouble, but is it possible to make him a few breakfast items, even if breakfast isn't being served anymore?"

Miles looked at Myrtle through narrowed eyes.

"Why sure, ma'am. The kitchen doesn't care. What'll it be, hon?"

Myrtle smiled. She liked that Miles got a *hon*, and that Myrtle got a *ma'am*. Pam was a smart woman.

Miles carefully detailed his perfect breakfast while Pam just as carefully jotted down every thrilling detail on her order pad. While the two of them were engrossed in this activity, a large man in his early forties with curly blond hair strode up behind Pam and quickly kissed the back of her neck, which was revealed due to her ponytail. Pam turned pink and whirled around.

"Steven!" she remonstrated at him. "I'm working!"

"Sorry, there's no place to sit or room for me to stand!" he said, looking very *un*-sorry. "And I'm coming off a twelve-hour shift." He wore an EMT uniform and looked tired.

Myrtle glanced at the door. It had become swamped since they'd walked in and was indeed standing-room-only. But there definitely wasn't even room to stand for a man this large. What was more, she had the sudden realization that this man must be Philomena's brother, the one who had given Amos the black eye. Puddin had said he was dating a waitress here.

"Why don't you sit with us while you wait for a seat to open up?" asked Myrtle, putting a polite and innocuous smile on her face.

Miles stared at her and then frowned in thought. He seemed to also realize that this was someone possibly connected with Amos. He scooted across the large seat to make room for the large man.

"Now, that's nice of you!" He sat down next to Miles and held out his hand in turn to both of them to introduce himself. "I'm Steven Fant."

"You must be exhausted if you've just come off a twelve-hour shift," said Myrtle.

Steven shrugged. "I am, but it's not so bad. I like the people I work with and I enjoy helping others, so it could be a lot worse than it is. I'll have a big meal and then go crash at home for eight hours."

The diner seemed to be clearing people out fairly quickly, so Myrtle felt as if she needed to get to the point before Steven disappeared.

"I think I know who you are," she said with a sweet, old-lady smile at him as though he were a favorite nephew. "You're Philomena's brother."

He raised his eyebrows and grinned back at her. "You're so right. Although I'm not sure how you fit those puzzle pieces together."

"Miles and I were just at the library. Miles has become fascinated with Sherlock Holmes and Philomena had the perfect book for him," said Myrtle.

Miles glowered at her. He apparently wasn't a fan of having his reading selections shared.

"Anyway, your sister mentioned that you were an EMT, and I noticed that you two favor each other," said Myrtle.

Miles snorted. And it was true that the statement was a stretch. Philomena was small and dainty and this man was a large bruiser.

Steven laughed. "I'm not sure that I've ever been told that before, but okay. We're both blond, I guess."

Myrtle's expression suddenly switched to a sorrowful one. "You might want to check in with her later ... maybe before you head home to rest. She had a shock, after all."

"A shock?" asked Steven, eyebrows pulled together in a frown.

"I'm afraid so. It was the news about Amos Subers," said Myrtle.

Their food was suddenly delivered, the timing of which irritated Myrtle. She didn't have the opportunity to see Steven's expression with pimento cheese dogs and a breakfast plate passing before her eyes.

When Pam had hurried away again, she saw that Steven's face was wary. "You were saying something about Amos?"

"Yes. He was found dead this morning—murdered." Myrtle speared a couple of chili-covered French fries with her fork.

Steven was quiet for a moment. Then he said, "Well, I'm sorry for his family and what they must be going through, but I can't say that I'm really torn up that the guy is dead."

Myrtle said, "What's your opinion of him? I was just telling Miles before we came here that I felt as though I didn't really know him at all—I taught him a long time ago, but people change from the time they're teenagers."

Steven's eyes were stormy. "I didn't think much of Amos at all, despite the fact that my sister was in a relationship with him. He had a smart mouth, which I didn't appreciate." He hesitated and then continued, "I might as well admit it, since you'll find out soon enough in a town this size. I popped Amos in the face about a week ago to let him know how *much* I didn't appreciate him. I felt bad about hitting the old guy, but he was pretty fit, so I ended up not feeling as bad as I thought I would."

Miles, who'd eaten most of the food on his plate, put his fork down. "It must have been hard to deal with Amos if you didn't like him. You must have been thrown into lots of situations where you had to spend time with him, considering your sister."

"I'd have thought that he and Philomena would have so much in common, too," said Myrtle. "Considering their love of books. Such a pity that Amos was difficult."

Steven said carefully, "They did share a love of books. And they were both what I'd call intellectuals. Philomena is the smartest person I've ever known, but Amos was sharp, himself. Just because I had issues with Amos doesn't mean that Philomena had issues with him." He frowned. "Before anybody in town jumps to the conclusion that *I* might have had something to do with Amos's death, they should talk to my manager. Like I said, I was working a twelve-hour shift with a paramedic to give me an alibi. I had nothing to do with it."

Myrtle said, "I'm sure no one will think any differently." Which was a complete and utter lie. "Who do you think *might* have been responsible? Since Amos was apparently so difficult, were there other people who had issues with him?"

Pam came back at that moment with Myrtle and Miles's check and a cheery smile for Steven. "Your table's ready, hon. Right over there in the back corner."

Steven gave her an absent smile and then said to Myrtle, "I'd imagine Alice Porper could be mad enough at Amos to knock him off. That's who I'd put my money on."

Then he got up and walked, arm-in-arm with Pam, to his booth.

Myrtle watched him go for a second and then turned her attention back to Miles and her plate. "Goodness, Miles, you must have been starving. This is the first time you've cleaned your plate at Bo's Diner. Or that you've finished before me."

There was not a morsel of food left remaining on Miles's plate. "I *was* hungry. That's what a frustrating game of Scrabble, in addition to investigating a murder, will do to you. Besides, you were the one doing most of the talking to Steven and you could hardly eat and talk at the same time."

Myrtle had polished off her chili fries but hadn't yet had the hot dog. She amended that fact immediately. "So let me eat for a minute or two and tell me all of your impressions."

"My impressions?" Miles looked as if his impressions might have had more to do with the quality of the food he'd just eaten.

"Yes. About Philomena and Steven. And Alice Porper, if you know anything at all about her." Myrtle took a big, satisfying bite of her pimento cheese dog.

Miles thoughtfully swished the ice cubes in his glass of sweet tea. He acted as though he was unaccustomed to the spotlight. "All right. Let's see. Philomena seemed shocked over Amos's death. Maybe she *is* responsible for it and was still in shock. It certainly didn't seem to be much of a premeditated crime since someone used a handy bottle of cleaning solution as the weapon."

Myrtle finished chewing and said, "And Steven?"

"He seemed overly protective of his older sister. There was quite the age gap there, wasn't there? I found it hard to believe that he gave Amos a black eye because he had a smart mouth. It seems most likely that Amos was, in Steven's eyes, somehow mistreating Philomena. Then he let Amos know in no uncertain terms that he was unhappy about that," said Miles.

Myrtle finished another bite of her food. "Yes, that's what I thought, too. He wanted to create some distance between Philomena and his own actions and maybe some distance between his sister and Amos, too. He was quick to point the finger at Alice Porper. All I know about Alice is from the years she's worked at the dress shop. Do you know her?"

Miles said, "She's the stereotypical 'woman scorned', apparently. Although I don't think she was angry, just hurt. They were dating for ages."

"I had no idea that you were so up on local gossip. I'm glad to know I have another source that I can go to besides Puddin," said Myrtle with a smile.

Miles said, "It's not gossip if it's something you witness in plain sight. Those two have been together for years. They were at the diner together. They went shopping together. They were at the movies together. They even went to church together. They were clearly a couple. Puddin even recognized Alice at Amos's house this morning."

"I must have missed the length of that relationship somehow," said Myrtle with a frown. "But then, I never pay much attention to who's dating whom unless there's some sort of a problem. Like Sloan, for instance. If there's a way that I can *help*, or if I'm interested in the people involved, then I suppose I look at it differently."

Miles said, "Anyway, that's what the situation was. Judging from the way that Alice was talking about Amos, I surmise that he broke up with her to go out with Philomena. And Alice wasn't happy about that at all."

Myrtle pulled out her pocketbook and paid for her portion of the meal. "Makes sense. We should see Alice next, then."

Pam hurried over to grab their dirty plates and their money.

Miles said, "How do you propose that we do that? Are we dropping by her house?"

"No, because she wouldn't be there. I might not know all the local gossip about Alice, but, as I mentioned, I do know where she works. She's always over at the women's dress shop in the strip mall in Centerville." Myrtle picked up her cane and her pocketbook and maneuvered around waitresses, busboys, and milling customers to make her way to the door.

"Lovely," muttered Miles. "We're making a trip to Centerville?"

"For heaven's sake, Miles, Centerville isn't on Pluto. It's a ten-minute drive from here. The next little town over." She walked through the door that Miles held open for her and carefully walked down the few steps.

"And what am I supposed to do while you're shopping for dresses?"

"They have a nice sitting area for men. It's delightful. It even has outdoor magazines there," said Myrtle. "Or, you can watch me shop and offer me advice."

"But you're just going in order to ask Alice questions about Amos, right?" Miles unlocked his car.

"Naturally, I want to ask Alice all about her relationship with Amos and where she was this morning. Puddin saw her at Amos's house, remember? But I wouldn't *mind* getting a dress while I'm there. My funeral dress is looking ragged. There are simply too many people kicking the bucket in Bradley," said Myrtle, clucking as she climbed in the car.

Fortunately for Miles, who didn't appear to want to spend much more time in the car, 'the other side of Bradley' wasn't all that far away, especially considering the size of the town. The brick edifice strip mall that the dress shop was housed in was an old one and also included a five and dime and an alterations shop. The dress shop's window showcased a couple of elderly manikins wearing linen dresses and large accessories and 'The Centerville Dress Shop' was painted on the window in yellow lettering and on the burgundy awning that covered the front of the shop. The door gave a cheery chime as they walked in. The carpet was a spotless green.

Alice Porper herself walked up to greet them with a smile. She was pretty, but an air of exhaustion seemed to hover around her, pinching her expression. Alice's blonde hair hung loosely around her face. "May I help you two?" she asked. She wore a nice dress herself, which was carefully accessorized with a turquoise necklace and earrings. Myrtle figured she probably received low pay but a good store discount.

"We're really not a *two*," said Miles hurriedly. He was always mindful of Bradley gossip. "I'm simply Myrtle's ride here."

Myrtle gave him an exasperated look and said, "You may help *me*, anyway. I'm needing a new funeral dress."

Alice blinked and said, "Oh dear. Anyone I know?"

"As a matter of fact, I'm afraid he is." Myrtle suddenly realized that she was delivering bad news for the second time that day. Drat Red for being so poky in his investigating! She glanced around for the men's sitting area and said, "Let's have a seat for a second, shall we?" Myrtle gave an apologetic old lady smile as if she couldn't bear her own weight for another minute.

Alice knit her brows, but obediently followed Myrtle and Miles to a tidy-looking sitting area with a loveseat and two armchairs. There were indeed a stack of hunting and fishing magazines on a coffee table in between the seats. Myrtle and Miles sat down in the armchairs and Myrtle waited for Alice to do the same. Alice hesitated for a minute ... perhaps she wasn't supposed to sit down unless she was on break. Then she quickly perched on the edge of the loveseat, smoothing her dress primly over her knees.

Myrtle said with a deep breath, "I realize this may come as a shock, but Amos Subers was discovered this morning. He had ... er ... passed away." She hazarded a glance at Alice to make sure that tears were not ensuing.

But Alice appeared to be more stunned than anything else. She didn't say a word, nor did she seem to be on the verge of crying. Alice continued staring blankly at Myrtle with those gray eyes.

Chapter Eight

Alice's shocked state alarmed Miles. He blurted, "Are you all right? Should we call someone?"

Alice shook her head and continued staring at Myrtle.

Myrtle took this as a sign to continue. She said, "Unfortunately, it didn't appear to be a natural death. I'm so sorry—I do know that you two were in a relationship for a long time."

Alice's silence became rather uncomfortable, which made Myrtle squirm. Finally, however, she spoke. "What happened?"

"Someone took it upon themselves to strike Amos with a glass cleaning bottle. I'm sure he never knew what hit him," said Myrtle. She wondered if she should change tack and give Alice time to process this information. Myrtle abruptly stood. "Let's talk about something more pleasant."

"Like your funeral dress?" asked Miles in a dry voice.

"Precisely," snapped Myrtle.

Alice moved quickly back into the role of shop associate. She stood and moved toward a rack of dresses almost as if from muscle memory. "What color dress were you wanting?"

"Nothing too lively," said Myrtle.

Alice was the type of store associate who had been in the business for so long that she knew exactly what size Myrtle was by looking at her. She glanced quickly at Myrtle's physique in an assessing manner.

Alice pursed her lips as she stared at the rack of dresses that were in Myrtle's size. She pulled out a black dress that had a large, abstract white pattern on it. Myrtle thought she heard Miles snicker from his chair. But when she turned to scowl at him, he was benignly reading from a fishing magazine.

"Perhaps something more traditional," said Myrtle.

Alice slid the dress back onto the rack and considered the dresses again. Then she said, "I know you said that you specifically wanted a dress for funerals. Are you sure you wouldn't like a top and pant? There would be more choice, for sure."

"Not sportswear, surely?" asked Myrtle in alarm.

Alice said, "Oh no, no. These would be dressy ensembles."

Myrtle squinted doubtfully. "Doesn't that violate some sort of funeral code for women of a particular age? I thought I had to wear hose, dark shoes, and a somber dress."

Alice said, "The problem is that we don't really *have* any somber-looking dresses. They're all party dresses. They're festive."

Myrtle blinked at her. "No dark coat dresses? Nothing suitably mournful?"

Alice regretfully shook her head, appearing quite remorseful over the store's shortcomings in stocking dreary, bleak garments.

Myrtle sighed. "I suppose I could use my old dress for occasions that seem to warrant something more formal and perhaps wear slacks and a top for others." She held up a finger. "*Only* if they're appropriately dressy."

Alice brightened. "I have just the thing." She walked farther away, navigating the circular racks that dotted the floor. She returned with a pair of black slacks and a black and white ¾ sleeve top with large black buttons.

Myrtle nodded slowly, head tilted sideways as she studied the outfit. "That's perfect, isn't it? It even covers up matronly arms."

"It's easy to wear, can be laundered at home, and is still rather smart-looking," said Alice. "Would you like to try it on?"

Myrtle remembered the calculating look from Alice when she was gauging her size. She had the feeling that the pants and top would be the perfect fit. "Oh, I don't think so. No, I'll just take them. Wait a second." She grabbed the dangling price tags and frowned at them before letting them go. "They even fit in my budget."

Alice smiled. "I kept budget concerns in mind when I pulled them out."

Myrtle followed Alice to a high counter in the front of the store. Alice was carefully sliding the pants and top in a garment bag when she paused. "Do you mind if I ask you more questions about Amos?" she asked tentatively.

Myrtle said, "It would only be natural. You must be so shocked to hear the news."

Alice said, "Honestly, I feel numb. I'm sure it will hit me soon and then I'll be positively devastated. Amos and I spent so much time together. He would plan special outings for us and we'd have such fun."

Myrtle said, "Amos certainly seemed to be quite the reader. Did he also enjoy the theater and art shows and so forth?"

Alice colored. "He did. I'm afraid that sometimes we weren't as good of a match in that department, though. I could get confused going to some of the films that he wanted to see. And I was hopeless going to see plays at the college—sometimes those were especially artsy. If we went to Charlotte to see art shows, those were completely over my head. I haven't had as much time to read as I'd like, either."

Myrtle raised her eyebrows. "It sounds as though you went out quite a bit together."

Alice gave a tinkling laugh. "It may *sound* that way, but these things were all stretched out over a number of years. Amos really didn't like spending money. Sometimes I'd even pay the way for both of us because I was under the impression that I had more disposable income than he did."

"But that wasn't the case?" asked Myrtle.

"No. Actually, I learned that Amos had plenty of money. He was simply something of a miser. He spent as little as he possibly could. I still treasured any small thing that he got for me ... but they were small. That's because I thought small things were all that he could afford. He'd bring me a single rose or a box of chocolates as surprises out of the clear blue. I always considered him so thoughtful," said Alice, rather sadly.

Myrtle said, "When did you discover that he had more money than you'd thought?"

"Oh, a few months ago. His daughter was yelling at Amos because *she'd* just discovered how much he was worth," said Alice.

Myrtle said, "That's right, he *does* have a daughter. What was her name again? I can see her in my head as clearly as anything."

"Josephine." Alice seemed to grimace when she said the name.

"Ah. And she's not very pleasant, is she? I'm remembering a thin woman with a perpetually unhappy expression and sharp features," said Myrtle.

Now Alice wore a faint smile. "That would be Josephine, yes. Frankly, I tried to spend as little time as possible with her, but it was difficult. She was frequently over at Amos's house."

"Was she? Did they get along well with each other?" asked Myrtle.

Alice shook her head. "Josephine was always upset with Amos and vice versa. Josephine felt as though she spent way too much time trying to *help* Amos. You see, he'd tell her that he needed some help around the house and she'd have to go over there after work or on weekends and help him with his laundry or scrubbing the baseboards or vacuuming, or whatever else he said he needed a hand with."

Myrtle frowned. "But he had a housekeeper. Puddin is my cleaning lady, too, and I know that she cleaned for Amos. Admittedly, she doesn't do a very good job and certainly doesn't do laundry, but I wouldn't think he would need both Puddin *and* Josephine to clean for him."

Alice said, "He only employed Puddin after Josephine refused to do any more work for him. She finally got fed up and took a closer look at his finances while he was out and she was in his house cleaning. She found his bank statements and investment statements and discovered that Amos was actually quite wealthy. And *that* made her furious at her father. Honestly, it made me pretty unhappy, too. I'd paid for some of our dates with my hard-earned cash, thinking I had more disposable income than Amos did."

"Is that why you broke up?" asked Myrtle.

Alice shook her head and flushed. She glanced in Miles's direction to make sure he wasn't listening in, but he had fallen asleep, his head lolling on his chest. "I didn't break up with Amos. Amos broke up with me. I was completely taken by surprise too and didn't see it coming. He was seeing someone behind my back. I felt so foolish and I had no idea that he was seeing Philomena. In a town this size! I must have been blind to it because I didn't want to know."

"And no one told you?" asked Myrtle. "No well-meaning girlfriend of yours? Because it's the type of thing that a woman would tell another woman if they were friends, isn't it?"

Alice nodded. "Yes, but you see, between working here at the shop and spending time with Amos, I really didn't have the free time to make or keep friends. So instead of people telling me that Amos was cheating on me, they were laughing at me." She looked miserably down at the floor.

Myrtle said briskly, "I'm sure that's not the case at all. They were probably reluctant to tell you about it because they thought it was none of their business. I certainly haven't seen any examples of anyone laughing at someone else in this town. Not adults, anyway."

Alice gave her a small smile. "Thanks, Miss Myrtle."

"What was your opinion of Philomena?" asked Myrtle.

Alice chuckled. "I suppose I can *try* to be unbiased, but no promises. She was probably a better intellectual match for Amos. He was always learning, always thinking. Philomena strikes me the same way. She's very brainy. We were in school together and she was always winning math club competitions and that sort of thing. But she was spoiled silly by her parents. I remember that she always wore the latest fashions and that they gave her a beautiful car on her sixteenth birthday. She always got what she wanted. I think all of us were green with envy."

"Have you had any conversations with her lately? Since she and Amos broke up?" asked Myrtle.

"Oh goodness no. No. As I mentioned, I think Philomena has always gotten whatever she wanted. And then, when she *didn't*, she wasn't very happy. The last couple of times that I've happened across Philomena at the drugstore or grocery store, she's given me quite the cold shoulder," said Alice.

Myrtle said, "That's silly of her. After all, it was Amos's choice whom to date. Do you have any idea who might have done such a thing to Amos? Who might have been unhappy enough with him to have murdered him?"

Alice's eyes were weepy now and Myrtle flinched. Fortunately, however, Alice appeared to get a grip on her emotions. "I suppose that *I'm* the prime suspect and the person who was the unhappiest with Amos. I wasn't happy when he left me for Philomena. But then, he did come back to me. I swear, Miss Myrtle, I was right here at the shop this morning. Really, I was!"

Myrtle said, "Someone, who might be wrong, mentioned seeing you at Amos's house this morning."

Alice's eyes were wide as she shook her head.

"Let's move past focusing on you for a moment. Who *else* might have been the person responsible for Amos's death?"

Alice said sadly, "I really hate to think like that. I can't imagine anyone who could be angry enough to kill Amos. I mean, Amos had his issues, but he sure wasn't the kind of person who gets himself murdered."

Myrtle gritted her teeth a moment before managing to ask in a pleasant voice, "But if you *had* to choose someone who might have been somehow involved, whom would you pick?"

Alice said slowly, "I'd choose Josephine."

Myrtle said, "His daughter was that unhappy that he had money and didn't tell her?"

"She was. And hurt. Plus, she has a terrible temper. Josephine even told me that *I* should step up and do more for Amos. That was before she realized that he was financially comfortable and didn't need anything else. She yelled at me like you wouldn't believe." Alice flushed again as if she was reliving the moment and it was just as painful as before.

Alice handed Myrtle the garment bag and said, brow wrinkling, "You don't think Amos was in any *pain,* do you? When he was murdered?"

Myrtle said, "He never knew what hit him."

Minutes later, Myrtle woke the sleeping Miles up and he made his stumbling way back to the car.

"Did you get that black and white splattered-looking dress then?" asked Miles. A smile tugged at the corners of his mouth. "It looked like a Rorschach test."

Myrtle glared at him. "It certainly didn't. It was a very fine dress, just not suited for me. I ended up with a pant and top combination."

Miles raised his eyebrows. "That's rather daring, isn't it? You usually have a set idea of the kind of thing you wear to funerals. I don't remember pants being in the mix unless you have some sort of wardrobe malfunction."

"I'm trying to keep up with the times. I'm surprised you're focusing on the fashion aspect of our visit with Alice instead of the interview aspect," said Myrtle.

Miles said, "Sorry. I dozed off in there. The outdoors magazine was hardly riveting. What did you find out?"

"I found out that Amos's daughter was not much of a fan of her father's. And that Amos had a lot more money than it seemed," said Myrtle.

Miles frowned. "He sure didn't seem to spend it. His house was very modest."

"That's the whole point. He was something of a miser and that's likely how he ended up with so much money," said Myrtle. "Apparently, his daughter used to clean for him before she found out that he could easily afford help. Then Puddin came on the scene."

"I have a feeling that a visit with Amos's daughter is on the horizon," said Miles as he drove.

Myrtle shook her head. "That's enough for today. I'd imagine that Red must have started with Amos's daughter, but I sure don't have it in me to inform another person today that Amos is dead, if not. We'll start out with his daughter tomorrow. Josephine, her name is. I want to go home and work on my piece for Sloan before he elbows me out of the writing of it. And I guess I need to transcribe Wanda's scribbles for him, too."

A few minutes later, Miles pulled onto Magnolia Lane and then in front of Myrtle's house. Staring out the window, he muttered, "What on earth? I don't remember your having such a large gnome in your collection. Is it new? What's it supposed to represent?"

"New gnome?" Myrtle glowered out the passenger window. "That's no gnome, that's Puddin! Why is she sitting in the middle of the gnomes? Plus, the gnomes aren't arranged *at all*, but thrown in a pile in the middle of the yard. Where's Dusty?"

Miles put the car in park and turned off the engine. They got out of the car and surveyed Myrtle's yard.

"I think that's Dusty there," said Miles, gesturing to a figure propped up against the wheel of his truck. Dusty appeared to be sleeping and Puddin, upon closer inspection, was most definitely sleeping as she slumped against two gnomes, her mouth open.

Myrtle walked over and positioned herself between Dusty in the driveway and Puddin in the yard. "What's going on here?" she bellowed.

They both jumped like guilty children.

Dusty glowered at Myrtle as if she was somehow to blame for the whole mess. "Back was thrown. Puddin had to help."

Puddin glared at Dusty. "Wasn't fair. Wasn't my job. An' I've had a rough day!"

Myrtle clucked. "Are thrown backs contagious? That's usually Puddin's excuse. These gnomes look horrid . . . and now what am I supposed to do? I can't leave them like this."

Puddin growled under her breath and Dusty said in a slightly louder voice this time, "Puddin' an' I'll fix it. My back's better after the nap."

"They don't have to be perfect, they simply shouldn't be in a pile in the yard," said Myrtle.

The two continued grouching as they lifted and moved the gnomes.

This being settled, Myrtle waved to Miles, who returned to his car and drove home.

Myrtle turned to Puddin. "I heard something very interesting about you today."

Puddin frowned at her and Myrtle continued, "I heard that you had an argument with Amos Subers at the library. And I have some questions about that."

Puddin said fiercely, "*Weren't* no argument. Just told him I wanted my money."

"Loudly? With a good deal of emphasis?" asked Myrtle. "In an argumentative fashion?"

Puddin tilted her head to one side to decode all of that. "I was mad."

"And what exactly were you doing at the library? You rarely hang out there," said Myrtle.

"I read!" said Puddin in a defensive tone.

Myrtle frowned at her and Dusty gave a dry cackle.

"I do! Went to your stupid book club, didn't I?" demanded Puddin.

Myrtle said, "You did. Of course, the meeting and discussion were already over and your attendance there consisted of bragging and eating leftover club food. Which takes me back to my original question: what were you doing at the library?"

Puddin continued stubbornly holding Myrtle's gaze until she suddenly dropped it. "Saw his car," she said sullenly.

"Amos's car? At the library? So you popped in to confront him," said Myrtle. "I do recall he had something of a distinctive car. A classic car, perhaps?"

"An *old* car!" said Puddin disdainfully.

"Well, it's most unfortunate that you chose the library as the place for your dispute. Loud voices stand out there and the library is popular on hot days. Now half the town probably knows that you had an issue with Amos directly before he was murdered," said Myrtle. She put her hands on her hips. "One other question, Puddin. You were acting very evasive when asked about your movements the morning of Amos's death. Where *were* you? You certainly weren't with Dusty."

Dusty nodded, staring at Puddin. No doubt he wanted to know the answer to that, too.

Puddin blushed. "Don't wanna say."

"If you want an alibi, it might be better to go ahead and spit it out, Puddin."

Puddin bit her lip, then sighed. "Played the lottery down at the gas station."

Dusty howled. "I done told you not to play it no more!"

Puddin gave him a defiant look. "Won last time, didn't I?"

"Won ten dollars. Spent twenty."

Puddin scowled at him. "Well, played it again. Then I got an Icee."

Myrtle sighed. "I'm not sure that's going to be a long enough errand to work as an alibi."

Puddin squinted at her. "But you'll figure it out. Who really done it."

"Of course I will. But in the meantime, be *cooperative*. Help me to help you," said Myrtle as she walked up to her front door and closed it behind her. "Complete and utter nonsense," she muttered to herself.

Chapter Nine

Myrtle walked into her kitchen and was greeted by Pasha, who bounded in through the kitchen window. "Good kitty," crooned Myrtle as she set out a paper plate with a can of tuna on it. Then she opened her pantry door ... and belatedly remembered that Red and Wanda had both wiped her out of pretty much anything interesting to eat. She'd forgotten to go to the store with Miles.

"Pooh," she said, staring into the pantry. She heard the front door loudly shut in the living room and called out, "If that's you, Puddin, those gnomes better be sitting pretty in the front yard!"

"Very threatening, Mama," drawled Red as he joined her in the kitchen. "But it's me." He shot her an irritated look. "Although I don't know why you elected to have your yard art pulled out. You and I have been getting along pretty well lately, I thought."

"Have we?" asked Myrtle coldly. She was *not* holding her cane, but this time that fact went unremarked by Red.

He looked exhausted and the small lines around his eyes were more pronounced. "Been a long day. Thought I'd grab something to eat before I head home and eat chia seeds or whatever."

Myrtle said, "That's fine, but you've apparently forgotten that you already wiped me out of most of the good food here and were going to go to the store for me to replenish it. But I suppose that murder has a way of being distracting."

Red slapped his forehead and groaned. "But Miles said he'd take you."

"We got busy."

Red said, "What's in the pantry to eat? I don't have time to run to the store now."

"See for yourself," said Myrtle, stepping aside.

Red frowned as he scoured the pantry for something edible. "I suppose I could eat Vienna sausages," he said doubtfully.

Myrtle said, "That's hardly a meal, Red. Are you sure it's not better simply to go home and eat dinner?"

"I'm sure," said Red in a fervent voice. "I don't know exactly what Elaine has planned, but I'm pretty certain it involves kale."

"I've enjoyed some excellent dishes at restaurants with kale as an ingredient," said Myrtle.

"Not the way that Elaine cooks kale," said Red. He surveyed the pantry again. "There are instant grits in there. I could cook up a batch of grits and cut up the Vienna sausages in it. That's practically gourmet." He looked sideways at his mother. "I could even make you a serving. It's either that or toaster pastries. I'm not at all sure why you have toaster pastries in your pantry. It seems an odd choice for an octogenarian."

"I bought them for Jack's visits," said Myrtle. "He absolutely loves them."

"And he runs all the sugar off after he gets back home, I'm sure." Red made two batches of instant grits and cut up the sausages for them.

A few minutes later they were eating. Myrtle said grudgingly, "This isn't as bad as I thought it would be."

Red grinned at her. "I can be a real chef when I choose to be. I'll try to go to the store for you tomorrow, Mama."

"Don't bother. You have the case to worry about. Besides, Miles will take me ... he never minds going to the grocery store." Myrtle scooped up another spoonful of the grits.

"That's funny. He never seems to want to run the errand when I hear him talk about it," said Red.

"Oh, he puts on a big show. But whenever he goes to the store with me, he remembers that he's out of paper towels or matches or bananas or whatever else he's overlooked. No, we'll be fine to run the errand, don't worry about it. We just got distracted today." Myrtle paused. "How are things going with your case?"

Red's expression turned sour. "You know, it's a funny thing about this case. Every time Lieutenant Perkins and I interview someone in connection with Amos Subers, it turns out they've all spoken with you and Miles already."

Myrtle opened her eyes in amazement. "Isn't that something! Who'd have thought? That's how things are in a small town, isn't it? You run into the same people."

"I don't quite buy the fact that you happened to have a conversation with Philomena Fant," said Red.

"How shortsighted of you, Red! You know how much time I spend at the library," said Myrtle huffily.

"Of course I do. But I'm also aware that you usually check yourself out at the circulation desk and don't ever communicate with the librarians," said Red. "You've frequently bragged how much faster you are at checking out books."

Myrtle said coldly, "Well, *this* time I was with Miles and we needed assistance. We spoke with Philomena about Miles's interest in Sherlock Holmes."

"Among other things," said Red.

"Naturally," said Myrtle. "One doesn't approach someone and ask for a book right off the bat. You engage in conversation first."

"And Alice Porper? She seems an odd choice for you to speak to, as well," said Red.

Myrtle said hotly, "Not if you'd seen the state of my funeral dress. I do declare, there are far too many funerals in the town of Bradley, North Carolina. My funeral dress is practically in shreds. Alice helped me find the perfect ensemble."

Red said, "Okay, Mama. You have an excuse for everything. But I want you to know that you're treading on thin ice with this case. There's a very dangerous person on the loose and I want you to make sure you're keeping yourself safe and sound."

"Naturally," said Myrtle in a cool voice.

"And I certainly hope that you're not writing any newspaper articles about Amos."

Myrtle said, "Sloan *depends* on me, Red, to write informative articles for the *Bugle*. I couldn't possibly consider doing otherwise. But I'm always prudent and thoughtful in everything that I take on."

Red sighed and rubbed his temples as if they were pounding. "I know what I meant to tell you, Mama. You know how you've always complained that Greener Pastures Retirement Home has horrible events and activities?"

Myrtle leveled a wary look at him.

"Well, you'll be delighted to know that they've brought on a new activities director who is supposed to be *excellent*," said Red. His voice indicated that the activities director had turned the retirement home into something akin to Disney World.

"The girls they hire there always treat the seniors as though they're preschoolers," snapped Myrtle. "I don't want to spend my precious free time reliving childhood games of musical chairs."

"Despite your gender-biased conclusion about the director, it's a *he*. And apparently, he provides quite a bit of eye-candy for the female residents," said Red in a persuasive tone.

Myrtle made a face. "If I'm unswayed by Miles's charms, and Miles is the hottest senior commodity in Bradley, then I'll hardly fall for a baby. That would make me a coyote, anyway."

Red frowned and said, "I believe you mean 'cougar.' But suit yourself. I just want to make sure you're not courting danger."

"The only thing I'm courting is a win in Scrabble," said Myrtle.

After Red left, Myrtle worked on the article for the *Bradley Bugle* and Wanda's horoscope. Then she quickly emailed them to Sloan. It was doubtful that they were in time for the next day's edition but would run the day after for sure.

Then she got ready for bed and read her book for a while. Myrtle didn't feel sleepy one bit, but it was definitely time to turn off the light and try to sleep.

Three hours later she rose again in irritation. Sleeping was apparently not on the agenda. Insomnia was a recurring issue. Fortunately, she knew that Miles shared the same affliction, at least most of the time. She would walk down to Miles's house to see if his lights were on.

Myrtle grabbed her bathrobe and her cane and walked out of the house. She kept an eye out for Pasha since the black cat had startled her before by leaping out of the shadows at her. Sure enough, she saw her move out of the bushes and jog toward her. The cat lovingly rubbed against Myrtle's legs.

"Good kitty," said Myrtle, reaching down carefully and rubbing the cat. "Want to visit Miles with me?"

Pasha gave every indication that she wanted to do so. She padded next to Myrtle as Myrtle walked, bathrobe swishing against her legs. They passed Erma's house and Myrtle held her breath until they'd safely cleared her property. The only nice thing she could say about Erma was that she was a good sleeper. Usually Myrtle didn't have to deal with Erma's antics in the middle of the night.

When Myrtle approached Miles's house, she saw his lights were indeed on. In fact, most of the house was lit up. She smiled as she walked up to his door and rang the doorbell.

Miles opened the door. "I have the coffee made." He stepped aside to let Myrtle in, grimacing as Pasha pranced in after her. "I'm not sure I have anything for Pasha, though."

Myrtle swept by him, heading for the kitchen. "You were expecting me, then? Have you been spending too much time with our psychic friend?"

"I've simply noticed a pattern where you frequently don't sleep the first night after a murder. As it happens, *I* wasn't able to sleep tonight after the full day. So I anticipated your arrival and perked the coffee." Miles followed her into the kitchen and opened a cabinet, inspecting the contents. "Do you think Pasha would care for canned salmon?"

"Always the thoughtful host. Yes, I'm sure Pasha would think she'd won the lottery if she had canned salmon. It's usually tuna at my house." Myrtle poured her coffee and added cream and a generous helping of sugar.

Miles eyed the sugar as he put a paper plate full of salmon down in front of an eager Pasha. "So you're not planning on turning in the rest of the evening, then? Judging from the amount of sugar you're putting in that coffee."

Myrtle shrugged. "I don't feel tired. And I'm having coffee, so there's probably not much hope of sleep, anyway. Maybe I'll catch some shuteye around 3:30 or so."

Miles watched as Pasha annihilated the salmon. "Maybe we should eat, too. Scrambled eggs? I think I have enough."

Myrtle said, "That sounds heavenly. I don't have any breakfast foods at home besides toaster pastries."

Miles raised his eyebrows and Myrtle waved her hand impatiently. "They're for my grandson. Anyway, I forgot that we were planning on going to the store."

Miles pulled out the eggs and scrambled them while Myrtle made toast. Soon they were eating at his kitchen table.

"What's our plan for today? Besides catching a couple of hours of sleep and going to the grocery store," said Miles.

"Josephine Mossom is the clear forerunner for interviews later today," said Myrtle. "She's the one that Alice thinks is responsible for Amos's death."

"Patricide?" asked Miles, making a face.

"It sounded as though she had legitimate issues with Amos," said Myrtle. "Anyway, she should be our first stop."

"Where does she work?" asked Miles.

"I believe she's employed by the fast food industry," said Myrtle. "Which is one reason she would be so enraged that her father had money when she was sharing her hard-earned cash with him."

Miles nodded. "We're off to the golden arches later? I suppose I can find a salad or something to eat there." His face was doubtful.

"Actually, I took the initiative to call them yesterday after I arrived home. Josephine is *not* working today. I suppose that she has taken the day off because of her father's death," said Myrtle. She frowned. "I sure would like to hear what was in Amos's will. I wonder who he left his money to. Apparently, he had a sizeable estate, despite how he lived. Maybe he left his money to Josephine."

"Which would provide another excellent motive for killing Amos," said Miles. "Not only was she furious with him for being duped about the state of his financial affairs and for cleaning his house, she might also be interested in getting a financial leg up by inheriting his estate."

"Right. So Josephine it is." Myrtle polished off the rest of her scrambled eggs and downed them with coffee.

"But how will we see her if she isn't working?" asked Miles.

Myrtle said, "We'll run by her house."

Miles raised his eyebrows. "On what pretense?"

"You were a friend of Amos's, Miles. Naturally you want to pass along your condolences to his daughter," said Myrtle.

"Friends? We simply played the odd hand of bridge or the occasional game of chess together. That doesn't seem much like friendship to me. It seems more like occupying the same space for a short period of time," said Miles.

"Which is good enough. And we'll bring a casserole over. She's grieving. It would be the nice, neighborly thing to do," said Myrtle.

Miles's face indicated that he wasn't sure it would be nice *or* neighborly to do so. "Look, we've already had a long day. We won't be operating on much sleep at all. I hardly think that your cooking, or mine either of course, improves with exhaustion. Why don't we pop by the store and pick up some ready-made food-stuffs of some sort?"

Myrtle frowned at him. "What sort of ready-made food-stuffs? Really Miles, that doesn't sound appealing at all."

"I've seen all kinds of things there. We could pick up a quiche, perhaps?" Miles looked anxious.

"Do you think Josephine Mossum is the type to enjoy quiches?" asked Myrtle doubtfully. "It all seems rather too much of an international flavor for someone in her line of work. Her palate is more accustomed to fried foods."

"All the better to change it," insisted Miles.

Myrtle said, "You seem quite passionate about this, Miles. All right, we'll pick up the quiche on the way over. Should we say ten o'clock?"

A wave of relief washed over Miles's features as he eagerly nodded.

Chapter Ten

At ten o'clock on the dot, Myrtle and Miles were at the grocery store. Myrtle dubiously surveyed the quiches.

"Are we sure Josephine will want a croque monsieur?" she asked.

"Just call it a ham and cheese quiche," said Miles. "And I've eaten these before—they're delicious."

Myrtle said, "Let's pick up aluminum foil while we're here to cover the pie tin and replace the plastic cover. I want to make it look as if I made it myself."

"And then refrigerated it?" Miles pointed out.

"I could have made it last night and then kept it in the fridge until we left," said Myrtle.

Back in the car, she quickly arranged the aluminum foil over the quiche, accidentally dropping the quiche in the process.

Miles pointed out that some of the quiche transferred to Myrtle's lap in the process. She opened the car door and brushed it out.

Miles said dryly, "I suppose the fact that it's broken makes it look especially homemade now."

"Precisely!"

Josephine lived in a modest apartment building a short drive from Bradley. When they rang the doorbell, she answered with a suspicious expression which quickly became tearful when she saw Myrtle and Miles and the covered dish.

Myrtle said brusquely, "Here, have a tissue, dear."

Josephine wordlessly motioned them to come inside. The inside of her apartment was just as modest and unassuming as the exterior but neat as a pin. Like her father, she was also a reader, although her budget apparently ran to used paperbacks. Either that, or she read the books repeatedly. As Myrtle peered at a crowded bookshelf, she noticed the books were arranged in alphabetical order by author. Josephine was a bit of a librarian, herself.

Josephine gestured for them to have a seat and Myrtle sat on an impeccably clean, if elderly, sofa. Miles, who for once didn't seem to have any issues regarding the cleanliness of Josephine's place, perched in an armchair. Josephine quickly put the quiche in the fridge in her galley kitchen and then joined them. She appeared to have completely recovered her composure. Myrtle thought she looked even thinner and frailer than usual. Plus, she seemed completely exhausted. Clearly, Red and Lt. Perkins had spoken with *her*.

"It's kind of you to come by," she said, holding out her hands helplessly. "I'm afraid that I didn't even realize you were close to my father."

Miles, who always had a hard time prevaricating, said, "I wouldn't say that I was *close*, but I played bridge and even chess with him sometimes."

Josephine raised her eyebrows. "Chess? That was brave of you."

Miles chuckled. "I only made the mistake of playing chess with him *once*. I didn't realize that a chess game could end so quickly. Amos checkmated me ten minutes in. It's like playing Scrabble with Myrtle."

Myrtle said, "It's nothing *like* playing Scrabble with Myrtle. We're having a very competitive game."

Miles's expression indicated that perhaps the Scrabble board would suffer another catastrophic fall in the near future.

"We're both so sorry for your loss, Josephine. Honestly, I'm still in shock from it all," said Myrtle, trying out her frail-old-lady act to see if it would work with Josephine.

It seemed to. Josephine said softly, "It was quite a surprise, wasn't it? And I understand that you and Miles were on the scene very quickly. Before the police made it there, right? That must have been distressing for you."

Myrtle nodded sadly. "It certainly was. You see, your father and I shared a cleaning woman. She'd cleaned my house before going to Amos's and apparently, I was on her brain. She called me before calling the police. Not that there was anything I could do. Who could have done such a terrible thing, Josephine? Do you have any ideas?"

Josephine slumped. "Unfortunately, Dad seemed to get on many people's bad sides. He could be pretty feisty. There are probably a few people that he'd recently made unhappy." She gave a harsh laugh. "To be honest, *I* was even unhappy with him in the weeks leading up to his death. I feel so guilty about that now—that we weren't on better terms."

Miles said, "But you had no idea what was coming. As far as you knew, you had plenty of time left with your father."

Josephine gave him a small smile. "Thanks for that. But even though I didn't realize how little time he had left, I shouldn't have held such a grudge against him. I mean, he got the picture that I was mad at him and I should have made up with him a within a week or so."

"What was the nature of your disagreement?" asked Myrtle. "Some things can be harder to forgive and forget than others."

Josephine nodded and then sighed. She said, "I had been helping my dad out for years. I thought he was basically living very lean. And he *was* living lean. The only thing he seemed to splurge on was books. He frequently even made his lady friends pay for dinner when they went out. I came over once a week to clean for him. The only thing he ever bought were books and that classic car of his."

Myrtle made a clucking noise. "And you didn't have much free time, yourself."

"No, not working where I do, and what's more, I always feel exhausted. But there are not a lot of job opportunities in a small town, you know. And when someone has found themselves a position, they usually hang on to it forever. There's no turnover. I've been divorced for years and there's no one else for me to rely on ... or so I thought. I've been stuck in this dead-end job and trying to help *him* out and even taking part-time jobs on the side when I could. When I realized that he was actually pretty wealthy, I lost it." She paused and looked wary. "I'll admit I was angry with Dad. But I had nothing to do with his death. I mean, why would I kill my father when he was all I had left of my family?"

Miles said in a comforting tone, "Of course you wouldn't."

Josephine gave him a tearful smile. "Thanks. I only wish the police agreed with you."

Myrtle said, "They think you're somehow involved?"

"Well, I don't have an alibi. I didn't think I'd need one!" she said with a harsh laugh. "And the truth is that I'm still pretty mad at Dad's treatment of me. I think that comes out when I talk about him. But aside from arguing over that one discovery about his money, Dad and I always got along fine."

Myrtle said, "I'm sure you did. Do you have any idea why Alice Porper would claim otherwise?"

Josephine's mouth turned down. "Alice never did like me. Somehow she seemed jealous of the close relationship that my father and I shared. Why on earth would I go over there and clean every week if we weren't close? We had one squabble and now I feel terrible about it because he's gone." Josephine stared at her hands, which were twisted together in her lap.

Myrtle said, "You said that your father got on people's bad sides. Is there anyone in particular you have in mind?"

"Well, now I want to name Alice, since she's apparently been saying things about me around town," said Josephine spitefully. "And that wouldn't be far from the truth. She and Dad had a good relationship ... until they didn't. But I won't tell tales. His cleaning woman that you two shared was upset with him because he owed her money."

Myrtle and Miles exchanged a quick look.

"In addition, I'll note that Dad and Gabriel Tharpe didn't always see eye-to-eye."

Miles raised his eyebrows in surprise. "Is that so? I always thought that they were the best of friends. I'd see them around town together having lunch or grabbing coffee. They always seemed to get along really well."

Josephine said, "There's a word for what they were. *Frenemies*. Are you familiar with it?"

Myrtle said, "Not really, but it's self-explanatory. I see. Friends and enemies."

"I'm not saying that Gabriel had anything to do with Dad's death," said Josephine in a rush as if Myrtle was about to phone Red. "It's just that they've been on the outs a little more than usual."

Miles cleared his throat. "Are there plans for your father's service, or is it too early to inquire?"

Josephine smiled at him again. "It's not too early. I received word from the state police today that there was no need for them to keep my father's body any longer—that his death was officially labeled murder by blunt force trauma. I'm hoping to bury him tomorrow afternoon; I've already been in touch with the funeral home." She gave them an apologetic look. "I'm afraid it's going to be a tiny affair—graveside only and that sort of thing. I don't have the funds to throw something really grand."

"Not that your father would have expected a grand gesture, I'm sure," said Myrtle. "I wouldn't worry about that. I suppose things will be better for you once the estate is settled."

"As far as I'm aware," said Josephine glumly. "I don't suppose Dad was cross enough with me to write me out of his will in the last couple of weeks."

"Surely not!" said Myrtle, aggravated by the very thought. "Not after all those years you dutifully cleaned for him. He wouldn't have dared."

Miles said, "Or, more likely, he wouldn't have wanted to pay the legal fee associated with such a maneuver. Having a will changed isn't exactly inexpensive, and it sounds as though your father wasn't much of a fan of spending money."

Josephine gave him a grateful look. "You're right. It doesn't sound like something he'd do. He was incredibly miserly."

"Even to the point of making his own cleaning products?" asked Myrtle. "Or was he making his own cleaners for other reasons—to ensure they were natural or green or something like that?"

"He did indeed make his own cleaning products, and only to save money. I don't think he cared a whit about the environment or using chemicals." Josephine made a rueful face. "He'd even fuss at his cleaning woman and me for using too many cleaning products. You should have seen his cleaning woman's face the first time he told her that!"

Myrtle could just imagine.

A few minutes later, Myrtle and Miles were back in Miles's car.

Miles said, "You know, I'd be mad too, if I were Josephine. That was thoughtless of Amos to make his daughter work so hard for so many years."

"And not offer to help her out! Instead, *she* was helping *him* out. Ridiculous." Myrtle squinted through the window. "Where are you taking me, Miles? Not home, I hope."

"Well, that *was* the plan. Don't tell me we're visiting Gabriel. How on earth do you plan on casually approaching him?" asked Miles.

"No, we're not seeing Gabriel today. I have hardly any scraps of food left at home and so we need to head to the store. As for Gabriel, we could simply say that your car was ailing. He owns a garage, I believe," said Myrtle in a careless voice.

"That sounds like a rather expensive excuse for talking with him," said Miles coldly. "Especially since there's nothing wrong with my car."

"Perhaps it needs a checkup," said Myrtle.

"It's a Volvo. It's in excellent condition," said Miles in a stiff voice.

"Maybe an oil change then," said Myrtle in exasperation. "Surely it's due for *something*."

"The oil for this car is very expensive and not due yet," said Miles. "It *could* stand to have its windshield fluid replenished. But I'd rather keep our going to Gabriel's garage as a last-resort. He and Amos were best friends. I'm sure that Gabriel will be going to Amos's funeral tomorrow to pay his respects, even if he and Amos had something of a strained relationship recently."

"I suppose that's true," said Myrtle. She didn't sound completely convinced.

"And if he's not, you could always tell him you're writing a story for the *Bugle* and wanted to get a quote from Gabriel about Amos," said Miles in a persuasive tone.

"All right, that does make sense," said Myrtle. "I do want us to talk to him, and soon. Despite his name, Gabriel is no angel."

Miles raised his eyebrows as he pulled into the grocery store parking lot. "It sounds as if you know more about Gabriel than I do."

"I mainly have suspicions about Gabriel. He was another of my students and was *constantly* in trouble. I had a hall pass for the principal's office ready and waiting for him every day. Modern-day Gabriel doesn't seem much better. He has a wicked smile. And he looks like he has secrets. People in Bradley have whispered about him for years—that he runs around with lots of women behind his poor wife's back. And Red has broken up several fights that Gabriel's been involved in over the years. Gabriel likes his drink," said Myrtle.

The grocery store was busy. Miles got a grocery cart and Myrtle, who was out of really everything, stopped every few feet to put in more food. Various neighbors and other acquaintances slowed their progress by chatting with them both.

Miles gritted through his teeth, "I'll never get used to living in a small town."

"People didn't accost you in the grocery aisles in Atlanta?" Myrtle tossed a couple of packages of dry pasta in her shopping buggy.

"No, they didn't. And they didn't study the contents of my cart and ask me if various products were any good, either," said Miles. "The good people of Bradley have a serious problem with nosiness."

"They probably think of it as product research," said Myrtle. "After all, why try something and hate it? Ask someone who's already tried it." She stopped walking and frowned, staring at a perfectly coiffed woman wearing white slacks and a silky black blouse. "Oh, pooh. There's Tippy. She has a bee in her bonnet over those garden club gala tickets. Perhaps we can avoid her."

Miles and Myrtle turned the cart around and strode rapidly in the other direction, but it was too late.

"Myrtle and Miles! What an unexpected pleasure." Tippy's voice called out from behind them. It was the kind of voice that couldn't be ignored.

"We could play deaf," whispered Myrtle. But Miles was already obediently turning around.

"Good to see you, Tippy," said Myrtle brusquely, although her tone stated otherwise.

Tippy beamed at her. "And how lucky that I ran into you, Myrtle. You're on my list of folks to call this afternoon. I need to check in with everyone to see how the ticket sales for the garden club gala are going. It will be such a lovely occasion and I want to make sure we have a great turnout."

Myrtle said, "I'm sure we will. Miles is thrilled about going to the gala."

Miles's expression was somewhat less than thrilled.

Tippy frowned. "Well, I'm glad to hear that, but I hope that you've sold more tickets than that. The gala is coming up in a few days and we've ordered a lot of food and beverages. And of course we want to give our speakers an honorarium."

Myrtle said, "I've sold quite a few of them, Tippy. Everyone seems to be looking forward to it." She crossed her fingers behind her back at the fibs.

Tippy said, "Wonderful! It will be a lot of fun." She checked her watch. "Looks like I'd better head out so that I can make those phone calls. Take care, you two. Don't get into too much trouble."

They heard Tippy's tinkling laugh as she walked away and Miles muttered, "I'm thrilled about the gala?"

"Well, you should be. It's an expensive evening of entertainment. Anyway, you bought a ticket so you should go."

"I bought a ticket because of your high-pressure sales techniques. I wasn't really planning on actually attending the event," said Miles.

"All the cool kids are coming. But if you don't want to be as cool as Wanda and me, I suppose you could stay at home and organize your sock drawer or clean your fish tank or whatever it is you'll end up doing." Myrtle put a packet of taco seasoning in her cart.

Miles said, "I don't *have* a fish tank, as you well know. Although you bring up an interesting point. I'd like to see how Wanda navigates the garden club gala. Have you considered the fact that she doesn't have anything to wear?"

Myrtle tilted her head thoughtfully. "She can probably dress up what she usually wears with jewelry or something. I could lend a necklace or earrings or something to her."

"There's absolutely no way her garments can be dressed up, Myrtle. I've never seen her in anything but the same two outfits over the years and they haven't improved in appearance in that amount of time. They're clean and that's all that can be said about them," said Miles.

Myrtle frowned. "I don't want her to feel uncomfortable at the gala. Maybe I can take her to the Centerville Dress Shop. That way I can check back in with Alice Porper while having an excellent excuse to be there."

Myrtle headed for the dairy section and Miles hurried to keep up with her.

He said, "That's an expensive shop. I'm sure it's not in Wanda's budget. And I'm not sure that buying another outfit there this month is likely in *your* budget, either."

Myrtle said, "It's pushing it. Especially with Red eating me out of house and home and with having to buy all my unsold gala tickets. Unless you'd like to contribute to Wanda's wardrobe fund? As a concerned cousin?"

Miles flinched as the family connection was mentioned and grimly nodded. "Yes. Let me know when you're planning on going and I'll send you with my credit card."

"I'm afraid you'll have to drive us there, too. Centerville isn't within walking distance and Wanda doesn't exactly have a reliable vehicle," said Myrtle.

Miles sighed. "I suppose I'll get reacquainted with the shop's hunting and fishing magazines."

Myrtle finished her shopping in record time. Miles drove her back and helped unload the groceries. "See you tomorrow for the funeral then?" he asked.

"Give me a call first thing in the morning and we'll work out the logistics," said Myrtle.

Chapter Eleven

B ut Myrtle didn't get a phone call first thing. She shrugged, figuring Miles must have slept in. She poured herself a large bowl of granola and then fed Pasha when she jumped in through the kitchen window. She was just putting on her new funeral outfit when the phone rang. It was Miles.

"Do you think Elaine can take you to Amos's funeral? I woke up with a raging headache," said Miles. His voice was subdued.

"If she can find someone to watch Jack for her. A funeral is hardly the place for a preschooler. But never mind that. Are you okay?" asked Myrtle.

"It's a migraine. I get them from time to time. I'm going to close my eyes for a while and hope it goes away," said Miles fervently.

"Good luck. Take aspirin, too," said Myrtle. "I'll check in on you later."

"Great," said Miles. His voice didn't sound particularly grateful, however.

Myrtle called Elaine and found that, fortunately, Jack had a playdate at a friend's house for the morning. And, despite whatever worthwhile tasks Elaine had *planned* on doing in that period of time, she was more than happy to drive Myrtle to Amos's funeral.

As usual, Elaine was cheerful as Myrtle walked up to Elaine's minivan.

"Myrtle! I love the new funeral outfit!" said Elaine. "Did you give your funeral dress the old heave-ho?"

"It was looking a little tired. I'm holding onto it, though. It can be the backup dress. It's good to have something else in the rotation. Bradley has so many funerals that I have to have something appropriate to wear."

Elaine reached over and quickly cleared off the passenger's seat, which held two organic granola bars, a small blanket, a canister of antibacterial wipes, a packet of travel tissues, a tube of sunscreen, a couple of sippy cups, and a few toy trucks.

Myrtle sat gingerly down in case there was any more preschool paraphernalia lurking on the seat below. Somehow, she'd thought all those things would have been in the backseat, near the car seat.

Elaine said, "Sorry about all that. Oh, and hey, let me know if you want to try this snack that I've brought. It tastes so amazing *and* it gives you energy and vitamins and minerals." She held up another zipper bag full of brown and black crunchy things of various shapes and sizes.

Myrtle was proud of the steady smile she was able to levy on Elaine. "Thanks, but I've already eaten breakfast. And I feel fairly energetic this morning."

"Well, it's here if you need it. Red *loves* it. And you might be hungry by the time we head home. I'm not sure how long

Amos's service will be." Elaine backed out of the driveway and drove at a fair pace down the street.

"Probably not very long, from what Josephine was telling me. She's somewhat short on funds and wasn't planning anything elaborate," said Myrtle.

"I didn't realize that you were close to Amos," said Elaine, giving her a quizzical look before looking back through the windshield. "Or is this more to do with the case surrounding his death?"

"The latter," said Myrtle. "For one thing, I'm trying to clear Puddin's name. She seems to be a suspect."

"Really?" Elaine's eyes grew wide. "Puddin? I mean, I knew she was the one who found Amos's body, but Red never really mentioned that she was a suspect. Why is that?"

"Oh, just her general foolishness. Threatening Amos in public in front of witnesses and that sort of thing. The type of nonsense you would expect from Puddin," said Myrtle.

"Why on earth would she threaten Amos? He was her employer!" said Elaine.

"Her employer who owed her money," said Myrtle. "Puddin is very particular about getting paid. Not so particular about showing up to work, definitely not as particular about the quality of her work, but most particular about receiving payment in a timely fashion."

Elaine shook her head. "Well, that's not good. And Red had mentioned that Amos was killed by a blow to the head from a glass bottle of cleaning solution?"

"Yes, he apparently hoarded money, even though he had a good deal of it. So he made his own cleaning solutions and didn't pay his housekeeper on time. Oh, and had his daughter cleaning for him before he even hired Puddin. He was a scamp," said Myrtle with a shrug.

"The type of murder weapon doesn't exactly help Puddin's case either, does it?" asked Elaine.

"Not so much," admitted Myrtle. "Although Puddin isn't the type to lose her temper to the point of hitting someone over the head. She prefers sulking."

Elaine pulled into the grounds of the new cemetery as opposed to the older one that was farther away. Here the plots weren't quite as well-kempt and there weren't the variety of different headstones as the other cemetery. It was more of the budget cemetery in Bradley.

Elaine drove around a few minutes to find parking. "There are more people here than I thought there'd be," she said. After a few more minutes she said, "How about if I drop you off near the graveside and then park the car?"

Myrtle, despite the energy she'd claimed to Elaine earlier, was more than happy to be dropped off. The day was a scorcher with temperatures already cresting 90 degrees Fahrenheit. A walk on an asphalt road to the graveside wouldn't be fun and might even mean her new funeral outfit would have to be dry-cleaned.

Myrtle approached the assembled mourners. In deference to her age, the crowd parted and a man who appeared to be the funeral director quickly suggested that Myrtle sit under the tent near the graveside. Myrtle, never one to look a gift horse in the mouth, plopped down in a folding chair under the tent. There weren't many people under it, despite the number of people at the service. Amos hadn't had much family and the tent space was usually reserved for close family. She saw Josephine give her a tight smile. Josephine looked uncomfortable in a dress that was most definitely *not* from the Centerville Dress Shop. She also wore rather too much makeup and, in testament to her distress, had mascara pooled under her eyes.

As suspected, Gabriel Tharpe was there. In fact, he was under the tent looking over some papers he held in his hands. It looked as if he might be speaking during the service.

Myrtle turned to look behind her and saw both Alice Porper and Philomena Fant standing outside the tent. They weren't standing near each other and each seemed to pretend that the other wasn't there.

There was no sign of Puddin, but that was hardly surprising.

After parking the car, Elaine joined the group standing outside the tent. When Myrtle motioned to her, she shook her head. Elaine was always one for protocol.

Apparently, Josephine attended church in a nearby town. A minister who Myrtle wasn't in the least acquainted with gave a rambling and rather nasal meditation until it was mercifully over. Josephine occasionally wiped tears away with angry swipes to her face. Gabriel was the lone speaker and delivered an eloquent eulogy in a deep, resonant voice. He spoke of Amos's love of books and reading and how often he frequented the library to expand his knowledge. There was no mention, perhaps purposefully, of his relationships with family or other people.

Following the service, Elaine met up with Myrtle as Myrtle was speaking briefly to Josephine, before Josephine was almost immediately pulled away by someone else.

"What now?" murmured Elaine. "Back home?"

This was said in a hopeful voice since Elaine had endured the blazing sun through the entire service and was now perspiring rather profusely.

"I did want to speak with Gabriel Tharpe," said Myrtle. "You could wait in the car if you wanted and blast the air conditioning."

Elaine raised an eyebrow. "You wanted to speak with him as a person of interest? I may hang around for that. After that eulogy, you'd never guess he could be a suspect in Amos's death."

Gabriel was one of those larger-than-life characters with lots of energy and an outgoing personality. As they approached him, he was speaking jovially to the minister who blinked at his enthusiasm and vitality—especially juxtaposed with the casket behind them. Gabriel's wife, looking tired, watched Gabriel for a few moments before heading to the parking lot.

When Gabriel spotted Myrtle and Elaine, he quickly ended his conversation with the somewhat relieved minister and turned his attentions on them.

"Well, I'll be. What a treat on such a sad day. My high school English teacher! Miss Myrtle, you know you were always my favorite." He gathered her into a hug, the type of hug where you fear the recipient might break.

Myrtle didn't like it when people assumed she was fragile because she was old. "I know you always had a golden tongue on you," she said briskly. "I do believe you're buttering me up, Gabriel."

"Never!" he grinned at her. His toothy grin reminded her of the wolf in various fairy tales, Little Red Riding Hood in particular.

Gabriel said, "And you've brought Elaine Clover with you, just to brighten up my day."

"Rather, the other way around," said Myrtle dryly. "Elaine brought *me* here."

She suddenly remembered that Gabriel was an irrepressible flirt. He appeared not to even be aware of what he was doing or prevent himself from doing it. This, as Myrtle recalled, led to all sorts of drama in high school where girls were concerned. She wondered what Gabriel's wife thought of his flirting.

Elaine, fortunately, seemed immune. "Nice to see you, Gabriel," she said.

Myrtle felt the need to commandeer the conversation and wrestle it back where she'd intended it to go. "You did a fine job with the eulogy. Amos would have been pleased."

Gabriel said, "High praise, coming from an English teacher. Thank you. I don't mind telling you that I broke out in a sweat over it yesterday. It's not every day that I need to stand up and talk about my best friend."

"You two were very close, weren't you?" asked Elaine sympathetically. "I know that I saw you both around town a lot together."

"We certainly were. And now I'm not sure who I'll end up seeing movies and plays with." Gabriel looked as pitiful as he could look, probably hoping that Elaine would offer to somehow fill the gap.

Myrtle said with a degree of asperity, "Your wife, presumably."

Gabriel grinned at her. "Jenny isn't one for going out much."

Myrtle switched gears. "Was it such a shock when you heard the news?"

"It was," said Gabriel solemnly. "I'd been working at the garage the entire morning, trying to get caught up on paperwork and motivate my mechanics to work faster. Honestly, I was beginning to think that I would have to pick up a wrench and start helping them. Anyway, that's when I heard the news ... one of my customers let me know. I left the garage immediately and took the rest of the day off. That's how shaken up I was."

Myrtle carefully said, "I know that my housekeeper, Puddin, was dreadfully upset by Amos's death because her last words to him weren't kind. Although, from what I've heard, Amos was a prickly old fellow sometimes. Were you both on good terms when he passed?"

Gabriel had a calculating look in his eye as he studied his former teacher. "We were the very best of friends, Miss Myrtle. Maybe there was an unkind word between us now and then, but even siblings fight, don't they? I was devastated. And everyone I know was upset just as much. Amos could be prickly, but he was still my friend. I'll admit that we had a tiff over something silly lately, but it was nothing that affected our relationship."

"A tiff?" asked Myrtle.

"Oh, something minor. We made an informal bet on the Belmont horse race. I didn't even think we were serious about it until Amos tried to make me pay up. I told him I'd only been joking and that I didn't have two hundred dollars to bet on horses. He stormed off and was mad about that for a while. But we were still the best of friends," said Gabriel.

Myrtle said, "Someone is covering up something. Because we all know that *somebody* was upset with Amos. Upset enough to murder him. I'd like to find out who that person was."

Gabriel raised his dark eyebrows and gave a delighted laugh. He turned to Elaine. "We have a Miss Marple on our hands."

"Miss Marple was a mere child," said Myrtle with a sniff. "I have more years of experience. Besides, I'm an investigative reporter for the newspaper. It's my job to get to the bottom of things and report on them."

"Then allow me to help you out," said Gabriel with a courteous bow of his head. "If I had to pick anyone who might be behind Amos's tragic death, I'd pick Philomena, our modest town librarian. Or perhaps her brother, who operates as her protector."

"And why do you think Philomena or her brother might be responsible?" asked Myrtle.

Gabriel grinned at her. "That's because Amos was a scoundrel. Not, naturally, something that I'd put in my eulogy in front of mourners, but let's face it. He had the morals of an alley cat when it came to women and he couldn't be faithful to save his life. He hadn't even broken up with Alice when he started seeing Philomena. Then he was supposed to be dating Philomena when he dated Alice again!"

Elaine shook her head. "He does sound like a scoundrel. Weren't both women furious with him?"

"They were, but they're both here today at his funeral. I tell you, Amos had a magical effect on women. They were furious at Amos, but you'd never guess it today. They're at his graveside wearing black and shedding tears," said Gabriel.

Myrtle said, "And Philomena's brother? It sounds as though Steven Fant wasn't too pleased about his sister being two-timed by Amos."

"He sure wasn't. Steven gave Amos a piece of his mind and a black eye not long ago and told him to stay away from his sister," said Gabriel.

"And you think he could have come by his house and murdered him?" asked Myrtle. She tilted her head to one side thoughtfully. "It seems odd, doesn't it? Weren't Amos and Alice back together? It's not as though Amos was bothering Philomena. He only broke up with her," said Myrtle.

Gabriel gave an expressive shrug. "Who knows? Maybe the more he thought about his sister getting dumped, the angrier he got. All I know is that Steven had already shown that he could be violent. I don't know who else might have done it. Anyway, I see that your son is on the case, so the bad guy will be in cuffs at any point now." He gave a lazy nod to indicate Red, who was looking their way with narrowed eyes. "I should go speak to Josephine. Good seeing you ladies." He gave that charming grin again and loped away.

Myrtle said, "I suppose I should have realized that Red would be here, but I didn't. I suppose I could have caught a ride with him."

Elaine said, "He was *hoping* to make it, but wasn't sure he could. Plus, he didn't go straight from the house. I'm glad he's here because I packed a lunch for him today and he forgot to grab it before he left. I put it in the car for him in case he made it here."

Myrtle hid a smile.

Red walked up a few minutes later and Elaine said, "How are things going?"

"Oh, we're making progress. Slowly but surely," said Red.

"I'm so glad I caught up with you, Red. I have your lunch in my car. I can hand it to you before we go," said Elaine.

Red flinched. "Thanks, Elaine. I guess I must have forgotten it this morning. Too much on my mind."

"Myrtle, are you ready to go?" asked Elaine.

Red said with alacrity, "How about if I take Mama home so you can run errands before you pick up Jack at his playdate? I thought I remembered that you have a few things you need to shop for."

Elaine said, "Are you sure? I thought you had a jampacked day today."

"I do, but I always have time to spend a few minutes with my mother," Red turned to Myrtle with a pleading smile.

Myrtle paused for effect for a moment, savoring the feeling of control over the situation. "Actually, that would be lovely. And I had a little chore that I needed Red to take care of, if he has five minutes to spare."

Red blurted, "I'm sure I can spare the time. And I'm done here, if you're ready to go now."

Minutes later, Myrtle was climbing into the front seat of Red's police cruiser.

Chapter Twelve

"It's nice that you're so eager to spend time with your mother," said Myrtle tartly.

Red said, "You have no idea what sort of fate awaited me in that lunch box. We'll have to dump it out at your house. Probably double-bag it before putting it in the trashcan."

"It couldn't be that bad. Besides, it's healthy. Elaine is looking out for you, you know."

"Looking to kill me, you mean," said Red morosely. He gave his mother a sideways look as he drove rapidly toward her house. "Why were you and Elaine talking to Gabriel Tharpe? Y'all are hardly friends."

"But I do know him. And I thought he gave an excellent eulogy today, and I wanted to commend him on it. I taught him years ago, remember?" said Myrtle.

"Years and *years* ago, yes. I thought you said he was a horrible student. He certainly wasn't one of your favorites, at any rate," said Red.

"No, my favorites were the students who actually did their homework and tried hard on the tests. Gabriel didn't exactly fit the bill. What frustrated me the most about him was that he was such a bright boy. A bright boy who wasn't making the most of his gifts," said Myrtle.

"I suppose he thought he didn't really *need* to use his gifts if he was inheriting his father's automotive garage. Which is exactly what happened," said Red. He looked at his mother again. "You know that Gabriel and Amos were good friends."

"Well, naturally. That's why he gave the eulogy," said Myrtle. She didn't offer anything else and fortunately Red didn't ask. Conversations about Myrtle's sleuthing usually ended up with Red making a reference to Greener Pastures retirement home. And Myrtle already had all of her gnomes pulled out.

The sight of the gnomes made Red clench his jaw as he pulled up into Myrtle's driveway. But he must have been ravenous indeed since he didn't say a word about them.

"You'll be glad to hear that Miles took me to the grocery store," said Myrtle. "Café Mama is now completely stocked with chips and sandwich meats and bread. Oh, and I picked up that pimento cheese that you always say you like."

"Thanks, Mama." Red actually sounded grateful. "And what fictitious chores are you having me work on, since that's our excuse? Just in case Elaine asks."

"How about unclogging my sink?" asked Myrtle.

"Perfect."

"No, really, how about unclogging it? It's not draining very quickly and I could use a hand with it. Maybe while I make you a sandwich?" asked Myrtle.

Red gave a resigned nod.

While Red was unscrewing the pipes under her kitchen sink, Myrtle said, "Now about this case. You couldn't possibly *really* suspect Puddin, could you?"

"Why couldn't I? People do unusual things under stress. Maybe Puddin's way of handling the stress she felt was to take it out on Amos." Red's voice was muffled from inside the cabinetry.

"What stress are we talking about? The stress of inventing excuses to get out of work? The stress of showing up on time? Because I really don't find Puddin's life remarkably stressful." Myrtle slathered mayonnaise on a couple of slices of bread. She sighed as she spilled mayo on her new top and pants.

"You know—the stress of asking Amos for money. Puddin clearly had a one-track mind when it came to getting her money. He wasn't providing payment, she became upset, she hit him over the head with a convenient cleaning solution bottle," said Red. He paused. "Do you have a small bucket that I can hold under this pipe when it opens up?"

Myrtle rummaged under another cabinet for a plastic container and handed it to him.

"That doesn't change the fact that you're talking about *Puddin*. Violence is not in Puddin's nature. To be violent, you need energy and aggression." Myrtle added shaved ham to the sandwich and then opened a bag of chips.

"Puddin is like everyone else. Pressure can make people do things out of character," said Red.

"But Puddin's way of responding to pressure is to take a nap in front of a game show. Which is likely what she was doing until she discovered Amos's body," said Myrtle.

Red carefully backed out of the cabinet and dumped the clog into the kitchen trashcan. "I don't know what to tell you, Mama. I certainly don't think that Puddin is a killer, but I still have to treat her like any other person of interest in this case. Puddin doesn't exactly hide her feelings, and she told me her opinion of Amos. It wasn't very good. I can't ignore that information."

"Well surely you're taking more of a look at someone like Gabriel," said Myrtle.

Red said, "And you were just saying how fond you were of him."

"I enjoyed talking to him, but I don't trust him as far as I can throw him. There's something he's hiding. I kept hearing that he and Amos had some sort of a split," said Myrtle.

Red was back under the sink again, putting the pipes back together. "That was probably simply the nature of their relationship, Mama. An on-again, off-again friendship."

"Or maybe it wasn't all that simple. Perhaps their problem was that it was more than a tiff, that it was something darker and more serious." Myrtle paused, trying to make her silence seem ominous. Perhaps Red wouldn't think that she was fishing for information. Perhaps he'd think that she *already had* it.

Fortunately, Red suspected the latter. He came back out from under the sink, washed his hands, and dried them off. Then he sat down across from his mother at the kitchen table. "All right. It sounds as if you've been sleuthing again."

"One doesn't have to *sleuth* to get information in this town. It's everywhere. It would be nearly impossible to avoid it most of the time," said Myrtle with a sniff. She waited.

Red took such a large bite from his sandwich that he pretty much devoured half of it in one bite. After swallowing and washing it down with some sweet tea he said, "So the town gossips know about Gabriel's indiscretion, is that it?"

Myrtle tried to keep her face completely neutral, despite the fact that she was hearing this news for the first time. "Naturally."

"Then why on earth did Amos think he could get away with blackmailing Gabriel?" asked Red, shaking his head. "That was stupid. And I think Amos was anything but stupid. The man had more books in his house than the Bradley library does."

"Well, sometimes even the smartest people can have stupid ideas," said Myrtle. "And Amos didn't seem to have a normal attitude about money."

"In what way?" asked Red, raising his eyebrows.

Myrtle smiled smugly. Apparently, she was ahead of Red's investigation. But, since he'd inadvertently shared some helpful information with her, she could do the same with him ... on a very small scale.

"He lived the life of a miser. Amos had plenty of money but hated parting with it. He was incredibly cheap in almost every way. He had his poor daughter cleaning his house for free and he didn't pay for his dates when they went out. It stands to reason that someone with this type of mentality might also be looking for ways to add to his money pile. Blackmail would be a relatively easy way of doing so," said Myrtle.

She saw that Red had already finished his sandwich and was halfway through the large bag of potato chips. She decided that she should make another sandwich or two for him or else she wouldn't have any chips left for later.

Red said, "I guess that makes sense, in a sort of twisted way."

"And clearly, Gabriel wouldn't want his wife to find out that he was having an affair. Although I don't think his wife would have been all that surprised. He's a natural flirt." She quickly made another sandwich and slid it over in front of Red.

"Is he?" asked Red.

"He acts like he can't even stop himself. But flirting is something completely different from actually having an affair," said Myrtle. She immediately started making a third sandwich.

Red said, "Gabriel would have felt he needed to keep his wife from finding out. But he isn't exactly loaded."

Myrtle put the third sandwich in front of him right as he finished the second. "I'd imagine he makes a decent income as owner of a garage, but I don't think he's sitting on a fortune as Amos apparently was. Maybe he was tempted to solve the problem by getting rid of his blackmailer."

"That's mere conjecture. And if people are saying that around town, I'd be sure to remind them of that fact." Red stood up and put his plate and glass in the dishwasher. "Okay, well, thanks, Mama."

"Did you get enough to eat?" Myrtle sincerely hoped so or else she'd be heading to the store again.

"I sure did. Enough that now I feel like a nap," said Red. He gave a yawn as proof.

"And Elaine doesn't suspect a thing?" asked Myrtle.

"Not so far. And at least this time your kitchen sink provided me with the perfect excuse for being here. I feel guilty, though—she's trying so hard and she's so excited to be making such healthy food for the family. I'm hoping she finishes up with this particular hobby quickly," said Red in a fervent voice.

"The hobbies never last long," said Myrtle. "Fingers crossed."

After Red left, Myrtle made herself a sandwich. She had taken the last bite when the phone rang. It was Puddin.

Puddin asked sullenly, "Does Red still think I done it?"

"You mean are you still a murder suspect? Yes, but I don't really think that he believes you're capable of it, Puddin. There's certainly no evidence or else you'd already be locked up by now," said Myrtle.

Puddin howled at the words 'locked up' and Myrtle pulled the receiver away from her ear.

"Is that all you wanted, Puddin? Because I really need to visit Miles. He had a migraine earlier and couldn't even make Amos's funeral. Of course, I noticed you weren't there, either," said Myrtle.

There was a pause on the other end and then Puddin said, "Didn't go to the funeral. Didn't like him."

"FYI, it doesn't help that you keep repeating that statement ,or words to that effect." Myrtle sighed. "I'm working hard to clear your name and you're working hard to undo what I'm doing."

Puddin said grouchily, "Okay, okay. Just called to get the name of a book."

"The name of a book? What do you mean? What book?"

Puddin said, "Told you I read books. But I need some practice. Tippy at book club told me to come back anytime."

"That's the kind of thing that people say when they're trying to be nice," said Myrtle. "Although you could go to book club with me. Why not? I'm already taking Wanda to the garden club gala. Although I'm not sure that you will like the book the club is currently reading. Besides, if you were planning on attending the next meeting, you should already be nearly finished with the book."

"I can read fast," said Puddin. Her doubtful tone contradicted the words. "What's the book? Does the library have it?"

"It's *1984*. They'd have it, but all the copies are probably checked out since it's this month's selection. Tell you what, I have an old copy from when I taught school. Although the book is covered with marginalia," said Myrtle.

Puddin's voice was suspicious on the other end of the line. "You mean like bugs?"

"I mean notes in the margins of the book," said Myrtle.

Another pause. "You *wrote* in the book?"

"It's allowed if it's your own book. Ignore the notes if they bother you," said Myrtle. "When do you want the book? And I'll remind you that you're going to need to do some speedy reading if you want to contribute at book club."

Puddin's voice was grumpy again. "Reckon I'll pick it up today. If Dusty's truck is workin', anyway. It's been ornery lately." There was yet another pause and then Puddin added, "Seems to me I should get to go to the gala, too. To be fair."

Myrtle said, "I don't know why I have to be fair. I'm not Wanda's and your mother, for heaven's sake."

Puddin was stubbornly silent on the other end.

"All right, I suppose you can go," said Myrtle with a sigh.

Puddin gave a satisfied chortle on the other end. "Okay. An' I'll get that book from you."

"Well, I may or may not be here. I'll leave the book out on my front porch for you," said Myrtle and then rang off abruptly.

It took her only a couple of minutes to find the book on the small bookshelf in her hall. The paperback's cover was soft with age and promptly fell apart in Myrtle's hands in surrender. She muttered to herself as she pulled some tape out of a drawer and hastily patched the book back together again and put it outside her front door. Then she hurried off down the street to Miles's house.

Myrtle was so caught up in her own thoughts of suspects, Miles, and *1984* that she neglected to see if her despised neighbor Erma Sherman was lurking around in her yard and ready to ambush her. And, as it was whenever Myrtle accidentally let her guard down, Erma was there waiting for her.

"Myrtle!" she shrieked, galloping over.

Myrtle jumped, startled, and turned her horrified gaze on Erma. Erma was grinning at her, showing her prominent front teeth.

"Going to see your paramour, I suppose?" Erma leered at her.

"If you mean my *friend*, Miles, then yes I am," said Myrtle in irritation. "He had a migraine today, and I wanted to run by and see if it was any better. So, if you'll excuse me?"

But Erma was never one to take a hint. "He didn't go to the funeral?" she asked, determined to keep the conversation going.

"No," said Myrtle, moving forward.

Erma hurried along beside her, increasing her speed to match Myrtle's. "Are you investigating? Like you usually do?"

"Naturally," said Myrtle. She sped up, making wide swings with her cane in the hopes that Erma would trip over it.

Erma said, "Do you think his girlfriend did it? Amos's, I mean?"

"Which girlfriend?" asked Myrtle, without being able to help herself. Erma, despite being annoying, did have both excellent eyesight and hearing and a willingness to snoop around and absorb all the local gossip.

"That Amos was a sly devil, wasn't he?" said Erma. She gave her annoying braying laugh. "I saw his girlfriend, Philomena, at the library when I was checking out the book club book. She was *crying*," said Erma importantly. She paused. "You might want to write this down, Myrtle. Your memory isn't what it used to be."

"My memory is *excellent*," said Myrtle coldly. She had a cold, sinking feeling hearing that Erma was talking about attending this month's book club. "You're going to book club tomorrow?"

"Not this time. I hated the book. I read the first three pages and then had to stop. *Anyway*! Back to Philomena crying. Of course I went over to see why she was crying," said Erma. She was huffing and puffing since Myrtle was still walking at a fast clip.

"Because you're so sensitive and you wanted to cheer her up," said Myrtle sardonically.

"Exactly. So I walked over and naturally she didn't really want to talk about it, but then I told her she would feel *so much better* if she did. That's when she told me how awful Amos was. That he'd made her think that they had some kind of future together and then ended right back with Alice Porper." Erma beamed at her. "That's important to know, isn't it? You can use that. Being mad gives her a motive."

"Thanks for that, Erma," said Myrtle between gritted teeth. It hurt her to thank Erma for anything. But it did prove that Philomena was more upset about Amos's lack of fidelity than she'd let on. Alice had hinted at much the same thing when she mentioned Philomena's icy glares at her.

"Say, what about your housekeeper? That Puddin. I heard that she was really mad at Amos, too. Everybody knows it because she was shouting at him in public. And, like we were saying, being mad gives someone a motive. You might have to find yourself a new cleaning lady!" Erma gave her braying laugh again.

Myrtle frowned sternly at her and then said firmly, "Puddin had *nothing* to do with it, Erma. That's something that you can do for me—spread the word that she's innocent."

Erma's face fell. "Oh, really? I'd thought it was pretty exciting if I had a killer right next door to me at your house. That would be something to talk about, wouldn't it?"

Ordinarily it would be nice for Erma to talk about anything but her own disgusting health problems, which were ordinarily her go-to topic of conversation. "Well, that's definitely not the case. So spread the word, like I said. I'll talk to you later, all right? I really do need to check in with Miles." Now she was standing in front of Miles's house and she did need to rid herself of Erma. Miles would never forgive her for allowing the woman to wander in with her when he had a migraine.

Erma said, "I'll let you know when I hear more clues!" She bounded away.

Myrtle rapped on Miles's door with great urgency in case Erma decided to extend their visit.

Chapter Thirteen

Miles answered. He was pale and his eyes squinted as if the sunshine hurt him.

Myrtle pushed her way past him. "Lock the door!" she said. "Erma may still be lurking out there or might remember something she forgot to tell me or something else equally horrid."

Miles immediately locked the door.

Myrtle walked over to Miles's sofa and plopped down. "Erma is so nosy and loud that I simply can't figure out why on earth no one murders *her*. All of these perfectly respectable people end up murdered and somehow Erma is always left in the land of the living. The murderers in this town are exceptionally dimwitted."

Miles carefully sat down in his recliner and immediately put it in the reclining position. "It's unfortunate. Thanks for managing to shake her off before she ended up in here. I couldn't have handled an Erma encounter today."

"I do bring good news. Erma is *not* going to the book club meeting. She didn't read the book because she disliked the first few pages," said Myrtle with a sniff. "Typical Erma."

"That's *excellent* news." Miles gave a wan smile.

"But the bad news is that Puddin has decided that she's a reader and is determined to crash book club." Myrtle made a face.

"Didn't I hear Tippy invite her, though? At the end of the meeting last time?" asked Miles. "She can't crash it if she was invited."

"Tippy only said that to be nice. I'm sure the *last* thing she wants is an obnoxious Puddin there. But I did give Puddin my old classroom copy of the book. After all, maybe it will distract her from making any more self-incriminating comments around town. Erma took great delight in informing me that the entire town believes Puddin is responsible for Amos's death," said Myrtle. She frowned at Miles's pale complexion. "How is the headache?"

Miles sighed and pushed his hands against his temples as if trying to offer himself some counter pressure. "It's much better but still somewhere in the background. I'm glad I didn't try to go to the funeral. I spent the morning with an icy gel pack on my face, lying in a dark room. The sun at the funeral service wouldn't have helped. Did you find anything out there?"

"I found out that Gabriel Tharpe is rather flirtatious. He was even flirting with Elaine as if it was some sort of compulsive reflex he had," said Myrtle.

Miles said, "That's chancy, isn't it, flirting with the wife of the police chief? Especially if you're a murder suspect."

"Like I said, I don't think he's able to help himself. That's why I wondered if perhaps Amos was blackmailing Gabriel over an affair," said Myrtle.

"*Blackmail*? When did blackmail come into the picture?" asked Miles.

"When I tricked Red into disclosing that fact. We knew that Gabriel and Amos had been on the outs, but we really didn't know why. Gabriel gave some sort of lame excuse about being irritated with Amos because Amos was trying to make him pay up on a silly horse racing bet. But I wonder if Gabriel had bragged to Amos about an affair and then Amos decided to hold it over his head and make him pay out," said Myrtle.

"It seems like an odd thing for Amos to do," said Miles.

"Amos was rather odd. Let's face it. He had a lot of money but behaved as though he didn't have any. This definitely would have been a way to supplement his income and also stick it to Gabriel. Maybe he *was* mad at him for not paying up after the horse racing bet," said Myrtle.

"Anything else?" asked Miles.

"Gabriel gave a lovely eulogy, but I suspect he's the sort of person who's able to fake it. Aside from that, he said that he believed Philomena or her brother must be responsible for Amos's death. And when I had my horrid run-in with Erma on the way over here, she said that she'd seen Philomena crying at the library and had harassed her until she confessed that she was crying over Amos and that he'd gone back to Alice. There were definitely some bad feelings there," said Myrtle.

Her phone started ringing, and she frowned as she pulled it out of her purse. Myrtle rolled her eyes when she saw who it was.

"Puddin? Did you find the book?" asked Myrtle.

Puddin's voice was suspicious. "Are you sure this is the right book?"

"It is."

"Didn't think y'all read history books at this book club," said Puddin, sounding sullen.

"History? No, we're decidedly not a history-reading book club. What makes you think so?"

"Because 1984 was a long time ago," said Puddin.

"Yes, but it was supposed to be a long time in the future. So you have to read it as though it's written about a time that's coming in the next hundred years or so," said Myrtle.

"This book is falling apart and has a lot of writin' in it," continued Puddin.

"Then leave it, for heaven's sake!" snapped Myrtle. "But you're the one who was so bound and determined to come to book club. Good luck finding another copy of the book. Although I happen to know that Erma Sherman picked up a copy from the library. She's not likely to be the kind to return it promptly, even though she has no intention of reading it. You could run by there and ask to borrow her copy."

The grumblings on the other end of the line indicated that Puddin thought a visit with Erma Sherman was not exactly on Puddin's agenda. Then Puddin said ungraciously, "Suppose I'll read yours then. Even though you wrote in it."

Puddin hung up and Myrtle sighed as she put her phone away.

Miles intoned, "I foresee disaster."

"That's Tippy's problem. She shouldn't have encouraged Puddin," said Myrtle, making a face.

"It seems to me that part of the problem is your own making," said Miles. "You're the one who implied that Puddin doesn't read books."

"That's because Puddin *doesn't* read books! She watches game shows and soap operas. Which reminds me, our soap should be coming on soon," said Myrtle, glancing at the clock.

Miles flinched as he frequently did when Myrtle used the words *our soap*. He enjoyed *Tomorrow's Promise* as much as she did but would rather keep it under his hat. The last thing he wanted was for the entire town of Bradley to know about his television viewing habits.

Myrtle stood up and put her hands on her hips. "Let's end this headache. It's getting tiresome. Have you had anything to eat?"

Miles shook his head.

"Have you had an aspirin or ibuprofen or anything in the last four hours?"

Again he shook his head.

"All right. So I'll make us sandwiches, give you some medicine, and we'll watch *Tomorrow's Promise*." Myrtle bustled away.

Ten minutes later, they were watching the show. Carmine had a secret baby that was turning out not to be secret anymore because Tristan was blackmailing her over it and she was trying to decide whether she should just let the knowledge be public.

After it was over, Miles said, "There's nothing like a soap opera to make real life seem dull and manageable in comparison."

"Exactly. Even though it's apparently full of blackmailing, too." Myrtle turned to look at Miles. "How are you feeling?"

"I think I'm back to normal," said Miles in surprise.

"Good. It's about time." Myrtle's phone rang again, and she scowled. "Is it that Puddin again? I swear I'm going to let her have it this time."

But it wasn't Puddin. It was Elaine.

"Everything all right?" asked Myrtle.

"Everything is all right here, but I have some terrible news. At least, it was terrible for *me* and I'm thinking it will be terrible for you, too. After all, we were both just talking to him!" Elaine sounded breathless.

"Who?" demanded Myrtle.

"Gabriel. He's been found dead!"

Chapter Fourteen

There was a wail on the other end and Elaine said hurriedly, "Got to go." She abruptly hung up.

Miles said, "What is it?"

"Gabriel Tharpe is dead. Jack is crying and Elaine can't give me any more information than that while he's upset. Let's go over there," said Myrtle.

Miles looked uncertain. "I've just successfully gotten rid of a migraine. I'm not sure that exposure to crying children is a logical next step."

"It'll be fine. He won't cry when he sees me," said Myrtle in a confident voice. They walked to Miles's front door.

"Why is that?"

Myrtle said, "Because he loves his Nana. And I'm a surprise visitor."

They crossed the street and walked down the sidewalk a little way.

Miles said, "Are we sure that Elaine would like a surprise visitor?"

"Maybe not at first. But she will after a few minutes," said Myrtle.

When Elaine greeted them, she was holding a still-wailing Jack. He'd apparently stumbled on the patio behind their house and skinned his knee, which Elaine had promptly bandaged. Jack's eyes were full of tears and sleepy and he clutched his blanket in both hands. When he spotted Myrtle, he stopped crying and held out his arms to her.

Elaine said quickly, "Let's let your Nana sit on the sofa and then I'll hand you to her."

Myrtle settled down and was soon holding a sleepy Jack who started watching a psychedelic-looking cartoon with his eyelids at half-mast while clutching a threadbare blanket.

"Wow, that was like magic," said Elaine. "Can you do that more often? Drop in anytime!"

Miles smiled in relief at the cessation of the loud crying. The cartoon with its odd mix of animation and puppetry seemed to be drawing him in with a horrified fascination. He sat next to Myrtle and Jack, mesmerized.

Myrtle gave him a small jab with her elbow to get his attention. "Now, about Gabriel," she said to Elaine.

Elaine's eyes grew big. "Isn't it awful, Myrtle? We just saw him, too. We were talking to him this morning and he was larger than life, like he usually is."

Myrtle said, "What exactly happened? Is it a natural death or foul play?"

"Definitely foul play. Red is working it with the state police. One of Gabriel's employees found him at the bottom of a steep flight of stairs," said Elaine.

Miles cleared his throat, pulling his gaze away with some effort from the television show. "He couldn't have simply fallen? Couldn't it have been an accident?"

"It was meant to look that way, but Gabriel was apparently hit on the top of the head with a tire iron, which caused him to fall down the stairs to begin with. The coroner immediately said that the original injury on his head wasn't caused by a fall," said Elaine.

Myrtle asked, "Since he was found by an employee, I'm guessing he was at the garage?"

"He was. The garage is on a steep hill and there are stairs leading down to the employee parking lot. I think those are the stairs Red was talking about," said Elaine. She shrugged. "But why would someone do that? It has to be connected to Amos's murder, doesn't it?"

"I can't imagine they're *unconnected*," said Myrtle. She gave Miles a little jab again as his attention drifted helplessly back to Jack's show.

Miles said, "I'd practically convinced myself that Gabriel was responsible for Amos's death, lovely eulogy or not. So I suppose I was wrong about that."

"It does seem unlikely," said Myrtle. She looked down. Jack had fallen sound asleep, still clutching his blanket.

"You have the magic touch today," said Elaine dryly. "He wasn't the same child before you walked in."

Myrtle said, "I'm sure it was the fault of that horrid child at his playdate. He shouldn't have made Jack overtired."

Elaine turned off the television. Miles, having lost his diversion, switched his attention to Jack and Myrtle. "Will Myrtle need to stay like this for the next hour or so, or can Jack be moved?"

Elaine said, "He can go right into his bed and won't even stir." Proving it, she carefully scooped Jack up, blanket and all, and carried him into his room.

She came back a minute later. "He'll feel like a new boy when he wakes up from his nap."

Miles said wistfully, "I wish I could have the same experience."

Myrtle said, "It probably helps that Jack *is* brand-new."

Elaine said, "Myrtle, did Red take care of your chore for you? Wasn't that why he was heading home with you from the funeral?"

Myrtle, without missing a beat, said smoothly, "Yes indeed. He fixed the clog in my kitchen sink."

"Did he eat at all while he was with you?" asked Elaine.

"Red? No. No, he was in a massive hurry to get away, like he always is. Why do you ask?"

Miles stared at her, marveling at the way the lies spun off her tongue.

"It's just sort of odd. I've been reading up on healthy diets and how they can really turn your life around. You remember the snack I showed you in the car?" asked Elaine.

Myrtle nodded, repressing a shudder at the unwanted memory of the proffered snack.

"I read how these diets can help you think clearly, prevent cancer, help with your sleep, and aid good digestion, and decided that's how I'd start preparing food in our house. But it's the craziest thing ... this healthy diet seems to make Red gain weight." Elaine shook her head. "I can't figure it out."

Miles's eyes were full of mirth and he quickly averted them as Myrtle gave him a disapproving stare.

"Maybe he's adding muscle. Muscle is heavier than fat," suggested Myrtle helpfully. In her mind she darkly promised herself that Red would pay for putting her in this position.

Elaine considered this. "Maybe if he was going to the gym every day, but he's been so busy that he hasn't been going. You don't think he's not finding the food *filling*, do you? That he's having to supplement what I'm feeding him? He didn't mention anything to you about being hungry, did he?"

Myrtle decided to give Red a little feedback for all the times he inserted himself in her business. "Hmm. You know, I believe his stomach growled while he was over, although he didn't eat anything. Maybe if you added more roughage to the diet you're giving him? Fiber should solve the problem."

Miles wiped his eyes which were streaming in his efforts to hold back laughter. Finally he gave a garbled excuse and hurried off in the direction of the hall bathroom.

Elaine stared after him. Myrtle said quickly, "Miles isn't quite over his migraine from this morning. I'm sure he's going to splash his face. Migraines make his eyes water."

"That's interesting," said Elaine slowly. "Is that a common reaction to migraines?"

"Only for Miles. He's quite sensitive about it. Perhaps we shouldn't look at him when he comes back," said Myrtle.

Elaine studiously looked away as Miles returned.

"We should be going," said Myrtle.

Elaine smiled at her. "You're amazing, Myrtle. You help Jack fall asleep and then you courteously leave because you know I have things to do while he's napping."

"I hope one of the main things you have to do is to put your feet up," said Myrtle.

"I'll put it on the list." Elaine hazarded a quick glance at Miles. "I hope you feel better soon, Miles."

Miles said, "Thanks, Elaine."

They walked out. Myrtle said grouchily, "I can't think why you lost it in there."

"Roughage," said Miles. The corners of his eyes crinkled again. "Red's culinary life will go downhill before it gets better."

"Don't worry about Red. He deserves every bit of it and more." She squinted at her house across the street. "Tell me that isn't Puddin at my house."

"I told you that having Puddin go to book club was a bad idea," said Miles.

But as they approached, Puddin didn't seem to have the book in her hand, which was a good sign. She spun wildly around, eyes huge as Myrtle called her name as they strode up the walkway.

Puddin clutched at her chest and snarled, "Shouldn't sneak up on people!"

"Who's sneaking?" demanded Myrtle. "You should have been able to hear my cane thumping on the ground immediately."

Puddin grabbed her arm. "Let's go inside." She glanced furtively around her as if worried there might be people spying on her from the bushes or behind the gnomes.

Myrtle unlocked the door and followed Puddin in. She rolled her eyes at Miles in anticipation of more nonsense.

Puddin said, "Red's gonna arrest me! Me and maybe Dusty, too."

Myrtle gave her a stern look. "Have you been reading *1984*, Puddin? Because it sure sounds as if you're paranoid about the authorities."

Puddin shrugged. "You said I had to read fast. It's scary."

"Yes, but the book and our town have little in common. You're perfectly safe here," said Myrtle in a tone that was meant to sound soothing but somehow came out bossy.

"But Red *is* gonna arrest me! I done gone to the garage." Puddin threw herself on Myrtle's sofa, being sure to put her feet up in the process.

Miles said, "You mean *Gabriel's* garage? Today?"

Myrtle said with a groan, "Say it isn't so."

"Today! 'Cause Dusty's truck done broke. I done told you that!" Puddin's eyes were bloodshot in her pasty face, providing a startling contrast.

Myrtle took a deep breath. "You did tell me that. I am aware that Dusty's transportation, as well as sometimes his yard equipment, can be unreliable in the best of times. But this is truly terrible timing, Puddin. Are you bound and determined to make yourself a suspect in this case? Now I have to defend you once again to Red and he's probably going to think that I'm only doing it because I desperately need you and Dusty to help me out around the house!"

Puddin glowered at her. "Didn't know he was dead, did I? Had to git the truck fixed."

"All right, so let's hear your alibi. And I really hope it's an ironclad one this time." Myrtle put her hand up to her forehead and wondered if migraines were catching.

Puddin squinted suspiciously at her.

Miles helpfully rephrased the request. "What were you doing today? All day long. We need to tell the police so that they'll know that you couldn't have murdered Gabriel."

Puddin thought about this. "Got up an' took a shower."

"Maybe in slightly less detail," suggested Miles, again most helpfully.

Puddin winced as though the careful curation of the day's events was painful. She apparently decided to skip eating and dressing and other things and finally said, "Dusty an' I wuz watchin' game shows."

"This morning?" asked Myrtle.

"Yep." Puddin gave her a defensive look.

"All of the cerebral game shows come on at night, you know. It's only the silly ones in the morning," said Myrtle.

Puddin glowered at her.

"Anyway, that's what we wuz doin', Dusty an' me. Then Dusty says that we gotta get the truck fixed. I said I wanted to eat first. Then I made a peanut butter sandwich."

Myrtle sighed. "Just the headlines, Puddin. I don't need all this detail. And how did you make so much headway with the book if your day was filled with eating and game shows?"

"I read fast!" Puddin gave her a scornful look. "Tol' you I was a reader."

Miles shifted wearily in his chair.

"All right, point taken. So, to recap, you and Dusty head over to the garage. And you ... what? Found Gabriel dead? Your second dead body in a mere matter of days?" asked Myrtle.

Puddin said, "He were already found by somebody else! The cops was already there. Red looked real suspicious that I was there again. Dusty tol' him about the truck."

"To be honest, Puddin, he has a lot to be suspicious about. You haven't been entirely truthful, especially concerning your altercation with Amos at the library," said Myrtle.

Puddin frowned at *altercation*.

"You had an argument with Amos," said Miles.

"And then you've been on the scene of two murders. No wonder you're looking guilty," said Myrtle.

Puddin fumed. "People say nasty things."

"Let's move on. In fact, let's *say* something unkind about someone else because finding out the truth is the only way that we're going to be able to get you out of this mess," said Myrtle.

"The truth will set you free," observed Miles.

Myrtle gave him an aggravated look to remind him that the best sidekicks were silent sidekicks.

"So who do you think killed Gabriel? And why do you think they might have done it?" asked Myrtle.

"Josephine!" said Puddin. She lifted her chin, looking self-righteous. "I bet he knew she killed her dad and then she had to get rid of him."

Miles embraced conscientious objection to being the silent sidekick. "You think Josephine killed her father and Gabriel knew about it."

"He was always around the house. Coulda seen somethin'," said Puddin.

Miles added, "And then Gabriel either blackmailed Josephine with the information or held it over her head."

"He was a tease," said Puddin. She flushed.

Myrtle sighed. If Gabriel had even flirted with Puddin, he truly had been a lost soul.

Puddin said, "And if the cops knew she killed her dad, she wouldn't get no money." Her eyes got big. "I better git my money from Josephine before she goes to jail. Can you drive me? Dusty has the car since the truck broke." She glanced around Myrtle's tidy house. "Do you have a baseball bat?" she asked.

Chapter Fifteen

"We're *not* going to Josephine's house to threaten her. Puddin, you don't have any sense. It's only going to make you look guiltier. Besides, Josephine wouldn't even have that money yet and we all know she can barely scrape two cents together," said Myrtle.

"Although it might be a good pretense for going over there and asking a few discreet questions," said Miles. "And technically, Puddin is a creditor. The executor of the estate should be paying her out for her ... how much did Amos owe you?"

"Fifty dollars!" said Puddin as emphatically as if she'd substituted *thousand* for *dollars*.

"Perhaps even Josephine has fifty extra dollars," said Myrtle. "At any rate, that's an excellent point, Miles. But Puddin, you need to stay as quiet as you possibly can and let me or Miles represent you."

"I'm going too? I'm not sure I feel comfortable about approaching the grieving daughter of a murder victim and shaking her down for cash," said Miles. He looked slightly green at the thought.

"We need someone to drive us over there, Miles. Puddin has already said their truck is incapacitated and I don't own a car," said Myrtle as if explaining things to a very small child. Then she beamed. "Never mind. I'll borrow your car. After all, you can't be expected to chauffeur me everywhere."

Miles shook his head emphatically. "No, thank you. I remember your last escapade in my Volvo."

"Escapade? How fanciful you are! It was no such thing—simply a little jaunt."

Miles said, "A jaunt that ended up with the vehicle stuck in a ditch."

"It wasn't a ditch. It was just a low point in the road that your car couldn't get out of. Really, if your Volvo was all that wonderful it should have four-wheel drive. I'm a *great* driver," said Myrtle.

Miles closed his eyes. "Just the same, I'll go ahead and drive us. But I'll stay in the car. I feel my migraine threatening to return."

"I suppose it *is* a very small place. Perhaps it would be better if you did stay in the car. We wouldn't want Josephine to feel threatened or get defensive with all of us there," said Myrtle.

A few minutes later, Miles backed up out of Myrtle's driveway with Myrtle in the passenger side and Puddin in the backseat like a rather wayward child.

"Better get my money," she kept muttering to herself.

Miles said, looking in the rearview mirror as they drove down the street, "Looks like Red is going into your house, Myrtle."

Myrtle swung around in her seat. "He has a key. I guess he's hungry."

Red spotted her and quickly pantomimed eating. Myrtle made a thumbs-up motion.

"I suppose he hasn't started eating roughage yet," said Miles, snickering.

"And *I* suppose Elaine must be taking a well-deserved nap now and that's how he's able to sneak over. I hope I have some food left when I get back home," fretted Myrtle.

Miles drove until they reached Josephine's apartment building. Myrtle and Puddin got out and Miles said, "Good luck. I'll sit here in the parking lot and read for a while."

"Your Sherlock Holmes book?" asked Myrtle.

"Finished," Miles said with a happy sigh. "Right before the migraine struck. Returning it to the library is on my list of things to do today."

"Glad that you won't be a fugitive anymore," said Myrtle with a smirk. "Just make sure you *do* return that book today. A visit with Philomena is in our future and I want my sidekick with me for that one."

"I put the book in the car," said Miles smugly.

Puddin was already making her way toward the apartment building, shoulders squared.

"You better wait for me or you're going to be asking a complete stranger for money," called Myrtle. "And I don't think the police will look kindly on that."

Puddin waited impatiently for Myrtle to catch up, hopping from one foot to the other like a child.

Myrtle said, "And remember! No being pushy. I'm here to make this process go civilly and smoothly."

Myrtle walked up to Josephine's apartment right when her front door opened. Josephine had dark circles under her eyes and wore her work uniform. "Oh, hello," she said in a voice that tried and failed to be welcoming.

Myrtle said, "You're on your way to work. Could Puddin and I take a couple of minutes of your time?"

Josephine gave a short laugh. "Sure. Usually I'd have to say no, but work has been unexpectedly accommodating lately because of my father's death. Is there something I can help you with?" She leveled a curious gaze on Puddin, who was watching them impatiently.

Myrtle gave Puddin a silencing look. "There may be. You probably didn't know this, but your father was a wee bit behind in paying Puddin, his housekeeper. It's been causing some consternation on her part and I told her that I'd help her reach out to you to see what could be done."

Josephine gave Puddin a sympathetic look. "I know where you're coming from. It's no fun scraping money together to pay the bills and even worse when you're owed money for work you've already done."

Puddin nodded vigorously.

Josephine said, "And it certainly sounds like my father to be behind on paying you. Now that I know the truth about his finances, he's the cheapest person I've ever met or even heard of."

"Cheaper than dirt!" said Puddin viciously.

"But the truth is, and it hurts me to say it, that you need to bring up Puddin's payment with Alice Porper," said Josephine, an exhausted tinge to her voice.

Puddin squinted at her disbelievingly. Before she could open her mouth to accuse Josephine of anything, Myrtle said, "Your father left his estate to Alice?"

"According to Dad's lawyer. He didn't leave me a cent," said Josephine bitterly.

"The house?" asked Myrtle.

"Also Alice's," said Josephine. "And I'm sure she's going to love to rub it all in my face. She never did like me." A stray tear trickled down her face and Josephine wiped it angrily away.

"Do you think this was an old will?" asked Myrtle. "Only because it seemed as though your father and Alice weren't all that close recently. Or, at least, that they were off and on."

"You mean because Dad was dating Philomena? I'd agree. Dad made the will some years ago, probably after some sort of small spat with me, and then he either forgot or was too lazy to get it updated." Josephine shrugged.

Puddin's face was splotchy red and Myrtle leveled a calming look at her. Myrtle said, "You could probably contest it. It might be worthwhile."

Josephine shrugged again. "I could, but with what money? That's also not exactly how I want to spend what little free time that I actually have. Besides, I only recently found out that Dad had any money at all—I'd never expected to get much. Although I suppose I thought I'd at least get the house and could leave my apartment."

Myrtle said, "On another subject, have you heard about Gabriel?"

"Yes, and that was about as shocking as my finding out that Dad had left me penniless," said Josephine. "I'm thinking his death was the result of bad karma. Gabriel didn't always treat people well and that obviously backfired." There was no small amount of malicious relish in her voice.

"Did he treat *you* well?" asked Myrtle.

"I didn't give him much of a chance to treat me one way or another. In my mind, he was Dad's friend. Not that he was the best of friends. He always seemed to bring out Dad's bad side. Dad would either start bragging around him or drinking too much or whatever. I avoided him and I avoided Dad when he was around him," said Josephine. "But I had nothing to do with Gabriel's death. I've been up to my eyeballs trying to plan the service and whatnot."

Puddin made disapproving noises, presumably about the drinking and bragging and not about the planning of the service.

"Do you have any idea who might be involved with his death?" asked Myrtle. "Do you think that Alice may be a suspect, considering he made her his heir?"

Josephine said, "As much as I'd like to think so, and even though I'm incredibly aggravated by all this, I don't think that Alice knew anything about it. The lawyer said she was as surprised as I am. But I don't know who killed Gabriel. Like I said, he wasn't always the nicest guy so it could be that he rubbed somebody the wrong way." She glanced at her watch. "I probably should go."

A couple of minutes later, Puddin and Myrtle were back in Miles's car.

"How did that go?" he asked. He appeared to be waking up from a short nap.

"He cheated her!" snarled Puddin.

Miles blinked.

Myrtle said, "Puddin means that Amos decided not to leave his estate to Josephine at all. Instead, he gave it to Alice Porper." She paused thoughtfully. "I think that was the most important information we received from our conversation."

Miles started driving. "Alice Porper! But I thought they weren't close anymore."

"Apparently he wrote the will some time ago and then forgot to change it," said Myrtle.

"Unbelievable," muttered Miles. "And Josephine is stuck in the same lifestyle."

"On the bright side, at least she's not cleaning her father's house anymore while trying to juggle work. And Josephine pointed out that she hadn't even realized that her father *had* any money until recently, so she doesn't feel as cheated as she might have." Myrtle looked out the window and saw Josephine driving away in an old-model sedan.

"Did she say anything about Gabriel's death?" asked Miles.

"Only that he had what was coming to him. She didn't seem to be much of a fan of Gabriel's and said that there were plenty of people who didn't like him and might have wanted to get rid of him," said Myrtle.

"An' she kept outta his way," added Puddin in a helpful tone.

Myrtle said, "She intimated that she avoided Gabriel whenever possible because she didn't think he was a good influence on her father and she didn't care for Amos's behavior when he was around him."

"Got it." Miles said, "Where am I driving, by the way? To the library? I hope so, because I really would like to return that book."

"So that you can sleep tonight with a clear conscience? I suppose so. I do want to speak with Philomena, and she's usually working during the week. Let's drop Puddin off first, though," said Myrtle.

Puddin said, "No way. I'll go to the library. I *read*, remember? Goin' to book club tomorrow."

"Oh, I keep forgetting that meeting is tomorrow." Myrtle groaned. "I have a feeling that it's going to be a nightmare."

"You can find me the next book to read," said Puddin complacently.

Miles said, "We might as well all go. The library is on the way to Puddin's house."

"All right, all right," said Myrtle grouchily. "But don't get too sidetracked. I'm trying to investigate, remember?"

The library wasn't nearly as busy as it usually was. It was frequently full of young mothers with children for story time, seniors getting computer instruction from a local volunteer, and students studying in groups or with tutors. Today there was only one dad and child looking for books in the children's section and a couple of older folks reading magazines in the lounge area in front of the gas fireplace. A fireplace that, mercifully, wasn't turned on, considering the temperatures outside were in the 90s.

Miles returned his book at the circulation desk and Puddin headed toward the shelves. Myrtle put out her hand. "Hold up a minute. You'll be in here all day if you approach book browsing that way. First question: do you want to read fiction or nonfiction?"

"Made-up or not made-up?" asked Puddin. When Myrtle nodded, she squinted in thought. "Made-up, I guess."

"All right. Then head over to *that* section. Because you were headed directly for the gardening books and I didn't want you to tell me that this library has boring books," said Myrtle. "Although, it wouldn't be a bad idea for *Dusty* to check out some of those books. What does he do in his spare time?"

Puddin made a face. "Drinks beer and watches racin' on TV."

"All right. Maybe we could check out some gardening *magazines* for him, instead," said Myrtle.

"Ain't you gonna help me find a book?" demanded Puddin. "Either one of you?"

Miles looked at Myrtle helplessly. "I don't really feel qualified to pick out something that Puddin might enjoy."

"Puddin, I'll definitely help you choose something, but I need to speak with Philomena first. Why don't you start looking through the books and I'll catch up with you?" said Myrtle.

Philomena, her blonde hair pulled back neatly in a tie, was putting books on the shelves from a cart. She smiled when she saw Miles and Myrtle approaching her. "How was that Sherlock Holmes companion book?"

"I've only just started it," said Miles. "I was finishing up another book first." Here he gave a guilty blush. "But it's great so far."

"Wonderful. I hope you'll enjoy it," said Philomena sincerely.

Myrtle said, "Did you get in touch with Tippy? Will you be at the book club meeting tomorrow?"

"She said they'd love to have me there. I'm nervous since I wasn't exactly prepared to speak so soon. I have my pick of topics: how librarians choose books, book recommendations, series recommendations, and so on." Philomena looked a little overwhelmed.

Myrtle said, "I'd be delighted to offer you some direction. Our book club adores classical literature."

Miles made a choking sound.

Myrtle ignored him, although Philomena pursed her lips as though worried there might be some sort of medical event about to transpire.

"The problem is that the club could use an expert to guide us and offer us some sort of direction. Perhaps some of the more entertaining classical novels would be best," said Myrtle.

"What is it that the club is reading now?" asked Philomena.

Myrtle beamed at her. She was delighted that her answer wasn't *Lost in Love* or some such beach mess. "*1984.*"

"Well, perhaps a good corresponding novel would be *Fahrenheit 451* or something similar," said Philomena looking more relaxed now that she had more of a game plan for her talk.

"That's a wonderful idea. And maybe you can help us plan out the following months as well," said Myrtle smoothly. She snapped her fingers. Perhaps *all* of her problems could be solved by simply spending time with Philomena. "Do you enjoy gardening?"

Miles rolled his eyes and looked longingly at the shelves of books.

Philomena said with a laugh, "Are you thinking about having me speak at your garden club, too?"

"Close. I was thinking that you might be interested in a ticket to my garden club's gala. There will be speakers and food. It's this weekend. It's supposed to be fun," said Myrtle rather unconvincingly, since she was not particularly excited about the event herself.

But somehow, she seemed to have interested Philomena. "As a matter of fact, I was thinking that I'd like to spend more time in my yard. Not today, maybe, while it's so hot outside. But I've been tinkering with my flowerbeds when I come home in the evenings and the temperatures have dropped some."

Myrtle said, "I just so happen to have a ticket left for this event. It's been very popular, you know. It's completely sold-out."

Miles again made a strangled sound.

Philomena said, "Do you mind if I get it? I don't have any plans for the weekend and I could use a distraction. My purse is right over there."

A minute later, she paid Myrtle and Myrtle fished the ticket out of her large purse.

"I hope you'll have fun," said Myrtle. Then she asked in a low voice, "Could you help me with a book recommendation for my friend, Puddin? She asked for my help and I can't seem to come up with anything for her. Her enthusiasm for reading may have made her rather over-confident in her abilities, unfortunately."

"What about a classic animal story?" asked Philomena smoothly. "*The Incredible Journey* or *Where the Red Fern Grows*?"

Both very sad books. Myrtle carefully weighed whether she wanted to deal with a tearful Puddin or not. She decided that any tears that the book may generate would likely be out of her presence. "Excellent idea," she said with a smile. Then she put on a sorrowful look. "I suppose you've heard about poor Gabriel."

Chapter Sixteen

Philomena's features became grim. "Yes. Yes, one of the patrons was talking about Gabriel's death about an hour ago. It's terrible to hear. I don't know what's going on in this town."

Miles said as if trying to make polite conversation, "It must have been especially upsetting to you. You likely spent a good deal of time with Gabriel, considering Amos and he were such good friends."

Philomena looked down as she put her gala ticket carefully into her purse and then put her purse on a shelf behind the counter. "Not as much as you'd guess. He and Amos weren't seeing all that much of each other at the time Amos and I were dating. There may have been some hard words between them or something. I never pressed Amos on it because he and I were having too much fun together to have another person tag along with us. Perhaps Amos wasn't seeing Gabriel because Amos and I were always at the bookshop or the movies or a concert. His wife is more of a homebody and didn't like going out as much." She paused. "Still, it's hard to believe he's gone, especially considering that we saw him at the funeral this morning."

Myrtle said, "You've had a busy day, haven't you? Did you go straight from the funeral to work?"

Philomena looked steadily at her. "Not exactly. The library gave me a half day off. I had lunch and then took a walk." She sighed. "That's the trouble with being single. You never have a good alibi."

Myrtle said, "Do you have any idea who might be responsible for Gabriel's death? Or even more ideas for who could have been behind Amos's?"

Philomena's voice, already Library Low, dropped even further. "I hate to bring this up, Miss Myrtle, especially considering she's your friend and that you've brought her here."

Philomena looked across the room and Myrtle and Miles turned to look, too. They watched Puddin who was gleefully grabbing books, looking at the covers, and then sticking them randomly back on the shelves.

"You think Puddin could be the murderer?" asked Myrtle. She couldn't contain a note of disbelief.

"As I said, I hate to bring it up. But you asked," said Philomena briskly.

"Why do you believe that she could be involved?" asked Myrtle. "Because I can assure you Puddin is a very simple person. Far too foolish to plan and execute two murders."

Philomena said, "She threatened Amos right in front of me, right here in the library. She was *most* disturbed about not being promptly paid."

Myrtle nodded. The fury of an unpaid Puddin.

"And who knows? Gabriel could have seen or heard something that made him realize that she was guilty. The same patron who told me about Gabriel's death also told me that your friend was at the scene of the crime once again." Philomena spread her hands out in front of her as if the case was closed.

That patron was certainly a loud mouth.

Miles said quickly, "She's coming over, by the way."

Puddin was indeed staggering toward them, holding a load of books. None of them appeared to be on the reading level of either *The Incredible Journey* or *Where the Red Fern Grows*.

"Got some books," she said in a satisfied voice. She heaved them onto the circulation desk. "This where I check 'em out?"

Philomena immediately switched to full-fledged librarian mode. "That's right. Did you find what you were looking for?"

"Found the same books Mr. Miles was readin'. Sherlock." Puddin smiled victoriously. "Him an' I go to the same book club."

Miles gave her a weak smile, likely envisioning Puddin calling him on the phone and demanding answers to questions about Sherlock, Watson, and whatever mystery they were embroiled in.

Myrtle said, "Well, anyway, it's all a huge pity. Two murders in a few days' time. And Gabriel was so full of life this morning."

Philomena said, "That he was. But I'm definitely not going to look at him as a better person than he was simply because he's dead. Neither will my brother." She stopped, as if irritated with herself for saying anything.

"Your brother Steven *did* get into a physical altercation with Amos, did he not?" asked Myrtle.

Philomena thoughtfully scanned Puddin's book and gave her a date due slip. "He's always very protective of me. He has been for years. He didn't care for Amos much and I don't think he liked Gabriel, either. But he wouldn't have had anything to do with their deaths because he works all the time. Amy, his wife, has had a lot of health problems the last couple of years and Steven has been working double shifts to take care of bills."

Philomena handed the book back to Puddin. "Hope you enjoy the book." She glanced behind them and said, "Sorry, but there are other patrons to help."

"Enjoy your afternoon," said Myrtle.

They piled into Miles's car and Miles drove away.

Puddin said pointedly, "The reason I wanted the Sherlock is because I'm doin' some investigating myself."

Miles and Myrtle said, "What?" at the same time.

"Told ya. I knowed who done it. Not gonna share it with nobody until me and Red talk."

Myrtle arched her eyebrows. "And you have a meeting set up with Red for this? The last I heard, you were terrified Red was going to arrest you for murder."

Puddin shrugged. "Sorta."

Puddin was many things and one of them was an inveterate show-off. Myrtle twisted around in her seat to look at Puddin and said, "You know you don't have the slightest clue. If you *did* know, you'd be quick to tell Red to keep suspicion off *you*."

Puddin grumbled from the backseat.

Myrtle's phone rang and she reached in her purse to pick it up. "Hello?" she asked impatiently, not recognizing the number that was calling.

"It's me," grated a scratchy voice on the other end.

"Wanda!" said Myrtle, pleased.

"Yep. Need ya to pass along somethin' to Puddin."

Myrtle didn't even blink that Wanda knew that Puddin was with her. "I'll put you on speaker, Wanda."

Myrtle fumbled with the phone while Puddin watched with trepidation from the backseat.

Then Wanda's ruined voice very clearly said, "Puddin. You is in danger." She paused. "That is all."

There was a click as Wanda hung up.

Puddin gave a great gasping breath and Myrtle said sternly, "You will *not* cry. I've had enough from you today. You need to stop bragging and carrying on and just hang out at home the rest of the day with your new book."

"An' skip work?" asked Puddin thoughtfully.

"Not the best idea. But maybe, depending on whose house you're cleaning, you *should* carry a baseball bat with you when you do," said Myrtle. "There is someone dangerous in this town."

They dropped a quieter and more thoughtful Puddin off at her house.

Miles said, "Where are we off to now? Food, perhaps?"

Myrtle sighed, "I suppose so. Let's pop by my house and have something there."

But when they drove up, they saw Red slipping surreptitiously inside Myrtle's house.

Myrtle said, "Drive on! I'm not in the mood to deal with Red right now and I'm sure he's not in the mood to deal with me."

Miles passed Myrtle's house and cut down another street. "I thought that you usually liked trying to catch up with him in the middle of a case. You like seeing if you can get some more information from him."

"Yes, but not right after a second body has been found. He'll be dashing in there to grab some of my chips or nuts or something extremely portable and then dashing out again. I can promise you that he won't find the time to say two words to me. Then he'll rush off to spend the rest of the day trying to talk to everyone," grumbled Myrtle.

"Sort of like what we're doing now," said Miles. "Minus the food."

"I'm starting to wonder if there will be any *left*," said Myrtle.

"Should I head to Bo's Diner then? It's really the only option, isn't it?" asked Miles.

"It's the only one that will afford you the opportunity to eat something at least nominally nutritious," said Myrtle.

"Albeit fried," said Miles sourly.

"Welcome to the South," said Myrtle.

As it happened, though, Miles didn't even make it all the way to the diner.

"Stop the car!" hissed Myrtle.

Miles obediently followed her directions after carefully putting on his blinker and slowly turning into a spot.

Myrtle said, "That's Steven, isn't it? Going into the fried chicken place."

Miles looked. "It sure looks like him. And he's with several emergency medical technicians."

"All right then, let's go to Clark's Clucks," said Myrtle.

Miles made a face. "Fried chicken is not exactly the healthy option that we were talking about. As I recall, this place has so much grease that it glazes the bottoms of the paper takeout bags." But he moved the car into a parking spot in front of the restaurant.

"It may not be healthy, but considering that we're dining with a team of EMTs, I think we'll be all right," said Myrtle.

"It also looks rather noisy in there." Miles pushed his glasses up on his nose.

"Is that migraine still toying with you?" Myrtle snapped her fingers. "You know, I can't believe that I didn't think of it before, but one of the helpful hints someone sent into the paper recently was that ginger ale can help with migraines. Except I don't think you're supposed to drink it if you're on a blood thinner. You're not on a blood thinner, are you?"

Miles said morosely, "Not currently, but who knows what sorts of health problems I might encounter after a meal at Clark's Clucks?"

"They have a variety of drinks here. You can get one out of their fridge," said Myrtle. She started walking briskly toward the restaurant with Miles following a couple of paces behind.

Compared to Bo's Diner, which wasn't exactly a fancy establishment, itself, Clark's Clucks was something of a hole in the wall. The aroma of fried food was noticeable yards from the door and was overwhelming inside. The interior was dim and crowded. Myrtle and Miles stood there for several moments, waiting for their eyes to adjust to the darkness.

While she was waiting and blinking, a deep voice said, "Miss Myrtle! Here, you shouldn't be standing. Guys, make room for Miss Myrtle."

Apparently, there were no such accommodations made for Miles, who was left glumly standing in a long line that reached to the door.

Myrtle knew when to play up her age. She said in a faint voice, "Thank you, young man." She peered closer. "Oh, goodness, it's Steven, isn't it? It's so dark in here that I didn't even see you at first. How have you been?"

"The question is more, how have *you* been?" he asked with concern. "Everything all right? I thought you looked a little weak when you came in. Need me to check your blood pressure or anything?"

Myrtle gauged this. She decided that she had Steven's attention now and that he might be more distracted if she let him check her vitals. "I'm all right now that I'm sitting. It's just the heat outside and the sun and then it was so dark in here. I was disoriented." She had been nothing of the kind.

Steven nodded in an understanding way.

Myrtle continued, "What's more, everything has been so very upsetting lately. It's really given me a turn. I suppose you heard about Gabriel's death? And right on top of Amos's, too."

Steven reached out and gave her hand a comforting squeeze. "I know you must get upset hearing about that kind of violence. And you probably hear a lot more about it than you need to, what with your son being police chief. But if it makes you feel any better, I'm sure you're completely safe here in Bradley. And what's more, I don't think either of those guys were all that great."

"Really?" asked Myrtle in an innocent voice that would hopefully make Steven elaborate.

"Really. I know you're not supposed to say bad things about the dead, but in my opinion, Amos and Gabriel were both asking for whatever it was that they got. I've been out of the loop a little because I'm getting off a double-shift, but if people are acting like they were super citizens of Bradley, then I'm telling you that they're just saying that because they're dead. Well, you know what I thought about Amos. I talked about him last time," said Steven. He glanced away for a second to check the line, which hadn't moved.

Miles, looking pale, flashed Myrtle an irritated look.

"But you really did feel the same about Gabriel, too?" asked Myrtle in that same sweet voice.

"I did. I certainly don't think that Bradley suffered a huge loss there. Oh, except for the fact that he was a decent mechanic and ran a decent garage. Aside from that, I gotta tell you that I didn't like the guy. And I sure didn't like the way that he treated my sister," said Steven.

Myrtle said, "You mean the way that *Amos* treated Philomena?"

"No, I mean the way that *Gabriel* did," said Steven in a distracted voice as a name was called for a table. It wasn't, fortunately, a name from his group.

"What did he do?" asked Myrtle, leaning forward. "For some reason, I had the opinion that Philomena and Gabriel didn't see much of each other."

"They certainly didn't, not after Gabriel dumped her that way." Steven's face flushed at the memory. "She had just started getting over Amos and then she was devastated when Gabriel ended their affair. For someone who was brilliant enough to go to an Ivy League school, my sister sure has a knack for picking the wrong guys." He looked uneasy. "Hey, you'll keep it under your hat that they were an item, won't you? She kept it a secret, of course. She worries a lot about her image in this town and what people think of her."

"Of course I will," said Myrtle, crossing her fingers out of sight.

He turned quickly again. "Miss Myrtle, the table is ready for me and the guys. You're sure you're all right? Your friend will be able to give you a hand if you need one?" He looked doubtfully at Miles as if not at all sure he was up for the task. Miles was looking around bemusedly as if pondering how he'd ended up in Clark's Clucks.

"We'll be fine, thanks. In fact, I don't think I have it in me today to continue waiting in line. I'll pick up a ginger ale for the road and we'll be on our way. Maybe I should hydrate more than eat," said Myrtle.

Steven smiled at her. "That sounds like a good idea, Miss Myrtle, especially in this heat. You take care, okay?" And he left to join his group.

Myrtle picked out a ginger ale, paid for it, and then gestured to Miles, who was still surrounded by throngs of people waiting for a table, to leave.

Chapter Seventeen

Miles pushed open the old wooden door with relief. Myrtle shoved the ginger ale at him. "Here. You should drink this for your migraine. You don't look so hot."

"It was the environment in there. It was too hot, too crowded, and too loud. I'm not thirsty now. Could you stick it in your purse for a while?" asked Miles as they got into his car.

Myrtle sighed and dropped the ginger ale into the depths of her pocketbook.

"What did Steven have to say?" asked Miles.

"Well, after he finished inquiring after my health, he told me that his sister had an *affair* with Gabriel for a time," said Myrtle.

Miles's eyebrows shot up. "I never would have guessed that."

"Apparently they must have kept it hush-hush since Gabriel is married. Her brother also mentioned that she was very conscious of what people in town thought about her. Steven, bless him, isn't discreet. Anyway, Steven didn't think much of Gabriel because he'd ended his affair with Philomena rather abruptly and she was still hurt from being dumped by Amos," said Myrtle.

"Do you think that Steven could have done it?" asked Miles.

"He was certainly angry enough at him to have done it. He's very protective of Philomena. But we saw for ourselves that he just came off a shift. With the nature of his job, he wouldn't exactly have time to slip away, commit a murder, and then hop back into an ambulance again. He's part of a team," said Myrtle.

Miles drove slowly toward Myrtle's house. "So Philomena lied to us. She said that she hardly ever saw Gabriel and that she avoided spending time with him."

"Either she's so used to lying about their affair that she's continuing to do it or else she has something to hide," said Myrtle with a shrug. "At any rate, we're seeing her tomorrow for book club."

At the mention of book club, Miles winced.

Myrtle said, "You need to have this ginger ale. I'm telling you, whoever sent in that tip for my column swore by it."

Miles said, "Not while I'm driving. Just hand it to me before you get out of the car." He paused. "You *are* getting out of the car, aren't you? We're not going anywhere else?"

"I still want to speak with Alice Porper, but I also want to make sure that I write an article about Gabriel's death for Sloan or else he'll find a way to bypass me and run a story himself. Let's worry with Alice tomorrow after book club," said Myrtle.

Miles said, "I don't even remember who is hosting book club tomorrow." He swung his head around and gave Myrtle a horrified look. "*I'm* not hosting book club tomorrow, am I?"

"No. Technically, it's Georgia's turn to host since she chose the book. But Georgia's home isn't exactly set up for a lot of guests. Too many knickknacks," said Myrtle.

"Not to mention that coffin she acquired at a yard sale that she uses as a coffee table," said Miles with a shudder.

Myrtle shrugged. "She said she wanted to find some practical use for it before she needed it. She said it was a real steal."

"I definitely can't see our dignified book club president putting her wine glass or tray of hors d'oeuvres on a coffin. Who's hosting instead of Georgia?" asked Miles. He pulled the car into Myrtle's driveway.

"Our dignified book club president is. Tippy offered. And Tippy is the one who coordinated with Philomena to speak," said Myrtle.

"And Tippy will be the one to deal with Puddin," said Miles. "This should be the most interesting book club meeting yet."

Myrtle gave a vague affirmation of that fact, but her mind was already writing the article for Sloan. She got out of Miles's car, set a time for him to pick her up the next day, and left with the ginger ale still in her purse.

The next morning, she had just finished getting dressed when there was a knock on her front door. She frowned. It was only seven in the morning. Myrtle peered out of her front door to see Red standing there, looking shiftily toward his house as if on the lookout for Elaine. Pasha was next to him, looking steadily up at Myrtle.

Myrtle opened the door to both of them and they both entered hastily—both asking to be fed.

Red said, "Didn't want to let myself in this early in the morning. Figured I might give you a scare."

"Is Elaine even up this morning? As I recall, she usually tries to sleep in until Jack wakes her up," said Myrtle. She followed Red and Pasha to the kitchen.

"No, she's not up, but I could hear that Jack was already stirring when I walked out the door, so it's only a matter of time. She left some sort of low-fat quinoa, raisin, and feta cheese muffins for me." He thrust a napkin full of napkins at Myrtle. "Can you get rid of them for me?"

Myrtle took them and sighed. "She's trying to make sure you're healthy, Red."

"Then why is she so obviously trying to do me in? She gave me a plate of kale and broccoli last night. And a bean medley." Red rummaged in her freezer and his eyes lit up when he discovered frozen bacon egg and cheese croissants. He dumped all the boxed contents onto a plate and put it in the microwave.

"Certainly sounds like quite a bit of fiber," said Myrtle as she took a can of tuna from her pantry for Pasha. The cat purred loudly as she brushed lovingly against Myrtle's legs.

"Roughage was the word that Elaine used," said Red, making a face. "She thought it would be more filling. Created all sorts of gastro distress."

Myrtle dumped out the can on a paper plate and lay it on the floor. Pasha, ravenous, attacked the food.

The microwave stopped and Red took the plate to the table and, equally ravenous, attacked his own food.

The feral cat and Red were on par to finish simultaneously. "You know, I have nothing against offering you refuge from Elaine's latest horrid hobby. But you should be offering me something in return. Half the time you're sneaking into my house and back out again when I'm not even here."

Red raised his eyebrows. "Keeping tabs on me? Do you have Erma Sherman acting as a spy?"

"As if I'd ever approach Erma about *anything*. No, but I've spotted you, as you'll recall. And there's evidence of a diminished food supply here," said Myrtle.

Red sighed. "I know, and I feel bad about that. But the truth is that I'm slammed at work right now. If people would stop getting murdered in this town, maybe I'd have a break. Right now, my breaks are consumed by paperwork, even when I'm not actively running around and gathering information. I'd go to the store and help you stock up if I had the chance."

"Then perhaps you can help me in another way," said Myrtle.

Red gave her a suspicious look as he took a final bite of a croissant. Pasha had proven herself the winner and was already languidly washing her face with a paw.

Red said, "I've already helped you with your clogged sink. Now what?"

"This time it's easier. I simply want a little information. Tell me how things are going with the investigation," said Myrtle. "And then perhaps one additional favor."

"You know that I can't talk about work," groaned Red.

"You're the police chief. You have the leeway to do exactly what you'd like. Besides, I'm asking for some basic information, that's all. A little direction," said Myrtle.

"And to know whether Puddin is still a suspect," said Red with a shrewd squint.

"It's just such a ridiculous concept. I can't imagine you're still entertaining it," said Myrtle. Pasha finished her bath and focused on Myrtle's face until Myrtle invited her up on her lap.

Red said, "You don't think that people have the capacity to surprise you anymore? I know you've been on this planet for a long time, but surely you're still up for surprises."

"On the contrary, people surprise me all the time. But there's usually only one surprise at a time. Puddin has already surprised me once in the last week." Myrtle scratched Pasha under her chin and the cat purred loudly.

"What surprise was that?" asked Red.

"She's attending book club with me this morning, having somehow read *1984*. And then she insisted on going to the library and voluntarily picking out a book to read in her spare time," said Myrtle.

"Was it a book about the history of game shows or soap operas?" asked Red.

"It was Sherlock Holmes."

Red scowled. "Although that *should* stun me, I'm sadly not surprised. I overheard some folks in the pharmacy saying that Puddin knew who'd done it. Which sure came as news to me since I haven't heard from her."

"Oh no. I'd told her to stay home yesterday afternoon and keep her mouth shut! I thought that Wanda had scared her a little, too. Instead, it sounds as if she's been bragging around town. She either keeps getting haplessly drawn into this case or else is playing at solving it. Anyway, this should absolve her from being a suspect. All of Puddin's mental capabilities are being challenged by trying to read and figure out who murdered Amos and

Gabriel. She doesn't have any room in her life for killing people," said Myrtle.

"She must be the unluckiest person I know, then. Puddin sure does seem to be on the spot whenever there's a serious crime," said Red.

"You know that Dusty's truck is falling apart. It's not surprising that she happened to be at the garage. It was simply unfortunate that she happened to be there when there was another body to be found," said Myrtle. "You're trying to distract me at this point. I still haven't received my information from you."

Red sighed. But he knew when he was caught between a rock and a hard place. He did still want to raid his mother's fridge. He did not want her changing the locks. And he knew that she was the type of woman to do it. He said slowly, "There's not a whole lot to know, Mama. Gabriel was hit over the head with a blunt object, most likely a tire iron picked up from his own garage, then a fall down the back stairs finished him off."

"So a crime of opportunity?" asked Myrtle.

Red said, "It was an opportunity of Gabriel's own making. We've heard that Gabriel liked to stir things up. He was fond of obtaining information and then holding it over the victim's head, just to make their lives stressful."

"Blackmail?" asked Myrtle.

Red shook his head. "Nothing even that elaborate. That was more like Amos. Gabriel liked teasing his targets with his information. Chances are, Gabriel figured out who killed Amos and was toying with them over it."

"Did anybody see or hear anything?" asked Myrtle.

Red said, "Not a thing. The mechanics on hand didn't notice anything, but then there are people milling around all the time, waiting for their oil to be changed or whatnot. And the place is incredibly noisy with drills and clanging and the guys yelling to each other. Plus, the mechanics liked working to loud music. It would have been a miracle if anyone had heard anything."

Myrtle said, "One more thing. What about Alice Porper's alibi? Did it check out?"

"What, at the dress shop? As it happens, Alice was running late that morning and had someone covering for her until she got there. So not the very best of alibis." He frowned. "You mentioned that you had something else you needed from me. Besides information."

"Oh, yes. You see, I've had all of these *expenses* lately. It's been rather hard on my retired teacher budget. My food costs alone have tripled," said Myrtle pointedly.

Red sighed and pulled out his wallet. "How much?"

"Enough to pay off the rest of these wretched garden club gala tickets and then some," said Myrtle.

Red carefully counted out bills before giving up and thrusting all of them at her.

"Thank you," said Myrtle sweetly.

He glanced at his watch. "Now I really have to make tracks before Elaine looks out the window and sees me over here." He gave her a serious look. "*Don't* go investigating this. There's a very dangerous person out there."

As he started walking out the door, Myrtle's phone rang. Red carefully locked Myrtle's front door and pulled it shut behind him. *Keep it locked*! he mouthed.

It was Puddin on the phone.

"So is Mr. Miles gonna pick me up, or what? You know Dusty's truck done broke," said Puddin. "And Dusty is drivin' my car now."

Myrtle sighed. "Are you *sure* you want to go to book club? I can promise you that I frequently don't look forward to our meetings. Tippy tends to pontificate when she hosts and Georgia is loud and says inappropriate things. The food is unremarkable."

"I done read the book! When will I get picked up?" asked Puddin.

Myrtle looked at her clock. "I'll call Miles."

Miles sounded as though he'd rather have a tooth pulled than attend book club. "Okay. We'll pick her up on our way to Tippy's."

"Not that it's on the way," muttered Myrtle.

"So I guess an extra fifteen minutes or so for you to be picked up," said Miles.

Puddin was sitting on her front porch when Miles pulled up some time later. She was wearing what appeared to be her best clothes since Myrtle had never seen them before and they had a new and untouched look about them. She was clutching Myrtle's copy of *1984*, which now seemed to be rubber-banded shut.

"Papers keep fallin' out," said Puddin.

A few minutes later, they pulled up in front of Tippy's large home. There were quite a few cars there.

Myrtle said, "You see what happens when we have a speaker? Practically everyone seems to be here."

"I just hope that Philomena can help give the club some good titles to read," said Miles.

Myrtle said, "Not that the club ever listened to *us*. But maybe they'll take it better coming from a librarian. Fingers crossed, anyway." She frowned at Puddin. "Make sure you don't brag about solving the case. You're making yourself a potential target for the murderer."

Puddin's eyes grew huge. "The murderer is at book club?"

Miles chuckled.

"That's not very likely. What's more likely is that everyone in this book club would gossip and spread the word that you know who did it," said Myrtle.

"Which I do," said Puddin, although not very convincingly. "Haven't been bragging, no how. Just told Bitty."

"Your cousin Bitty has the biggest mouth in Bradley," said Myrtle.

Puddin muttered under her breath as they walked in.

There were indeed a lot of people in attendance at book club. Myrtle was sure she hadn't seen Sherry or Blanche at book club for a while. Georgia was there and was already talking about the book, which was a club no-no. Tippy was directing people to food and beverages while speaking with Philomena.

Miles was, of course, quickly whisked away from Myrtle. He was extremely popular with the book club and the ladies flirted mercilessly with him. Myrtle found herself in a conversation with Sherry in which Sherry tried to convince her that she was missing out on group yoga at the fitness center. Myrtle was quite sure that she wasn't missing a thing.

Finally, it was time for the meeting to start. Miles sat down next to Myrtle.

Miles said, "I can't wait to see what Georgia thought of *1984*. Especially since it was her pick."

Myrtle glanced at Georgia. Georgia was something of an anomaly in the club, although certainly not as much of an anomaly as Puddin was today. She was covered with tattoos, collected ceramic angels, trolled yard sales, swore like a sailor, and apparently reminded Miles of someone he had served in Vietnam with.

"I think you want to hear what Georgia thinks because of your secret crush on her," said Myrtle, not doing a good job suppressing a smile.

Miles changed the subject. "Why isn't Puddin sitting over here with us? I thought she'd want to hover nearby. She doesn't know most of these women."

"Only because they can afford better housekeepers. But I'm sure her cousin Bitty keeps her informed about all of these women considering the gossip queen that she is. Puddin likely knows more about them than we do," said Myrtle. "And I'm pretty certain that Puddin is trying to prove a point by sitting over there with Tippy. She was quite offended by my supposition that she was not a reader."

Tippy was still going over club business and asking for the minutes of the last meeting. Miles said in an undertone, "I still say this will be a disaster no matter what. On the one hand, Puddin will spew some complete nonsense about the book."

"Which will put her on the same level as most of the other women in the club," pointed out Myrtle. "Remember when Erma thought that *To Kill a Mockingbird* was about Girl Scouts?"

Miles continued, "Or, on the other hand, she'll wisely keep her mouth shut and will continue returning to book club on a regular basis."

"Which we *do not want*," said Myrtle. "I can't handle more exposure to Puddin than I get from having her clean for me."

"Did she call you up and ask you a million questions about *1984*?" asked Miles.

"Oddly, no. Except that she mistakenly thought that it was a historical novel of some sort, because of the title," said Myrtle. She frowned in irritation and then hissed to Miles, "Why on earth do we have to suffer through the minutes of the previous meeting? Do we really need a recap of eating pimento cheese sandwiches and drinking iced tea?"

After another excruciating wait through the rest of the minutes that were painstakingly read by the painfully shy and timid Margaret Goodner, it was time to start discussing the book.

Georgia, as the person who'd proposed the book, started the conversation. Usually the club members stayed seated and talked about the book in a round robin manner. Georgia decided to break with tradition and stood up, walking restlessly around.

In her loud voice, she said, "I know I picked this selection, but boy, this book is messed up!"

Chapter Eighteen

The ladies tittered nervously. Georgia always seemed explosive and they never really knew when the explosion was going to happen.

She continued, "I mean . . . it was good and everything. I liked the theme pretty well. I get that it was meant to be a cautionary tale. But wow. It wasn't exactly a feel-good read, was it?"

Apparently, that's all that Georgia had to say about it. Myrtle frowned. Georgia was one of the few members who had ever proposed anything remotely literary at the club. It simply wouldn't do if Georgia gave up at this point. Myrtle saw Philomena looking in her direction and mouthed, "Help!" at her.

Philomena said cautiously, "Reading the classics can be tough, can't it? Sometimes these books won't have the happy endings that we've gotten used to with commercial fiction."

The nervous tittering stopped and there were some discontented murmurs taking their place. Happy endings were, for this particular book club, what the entire reading experience was all about. Tippy, a consummate hostess, looked nervous. She was no fan of discord.

Tippy cleared her throat and said, "And, for those of you who haven't had the pleasure of meeting her, this is Philomena Fant. Philomena is a librarian and has graciously agreed to be our speaker today."

The club members put on their polite neutral faces. They could tell when Tippy wasn't pleased and none of them wanted to be on Tippy's bad side since she was very influential in the town.

Puddin, however, did not seem to be picking up on any messages at all. She said, "Yeah, but it ain't fun sometimes to read them kinds of stories."

Miles murmured to Myrtle, "Eloquently stated."

The members murmured in agreement with Puddin as Tippy tried to maintain control of the meeting. "Let's see. I think we'll start going around in a circle with everyone talking a few minutes and giving their thoughts on the book. Puddin, why don't you go first?" Tippy smiled at the assembled readers and said, "And for those who haven't met Puddin, this is Puddin . . . ." She paused for a last name and, not getting one, said, "Puddin."

"Here we go," said Miles under his breath. He seemed to be bracing himself.

Puddin, like Georgia, decided to stand up. She swaggered, giving a beneficent, condescending grin to each of the women as if about to impart some sort of literary wisdom on all of them.

"This will be bad," said Miles.

Puddin said, "It was a good book. Like she said," gesturing to Georgia, "it coulda been better. But there was them symbols and things."

Myrtle frowned. Puddin was noticing symbols?

"Stuff like that glass paperweight that Winston got. You might think it was just a glass paperweight an' that was *it*," said Puddin.

Tippy frowned as if she'd either skimmed over the glass paperweight parts or had taken them at face value.

Miles whispered, "What's going on here?"

Myrtle sighed. "I think it's my marginalia in the book. It was my copy of *1984* that I taught for school and all of my notes for class were in there."

"Well, she's going to sound like a genius compared to everyone else," said Miles.

Myrtle said, "And you know what it's like when she gets attention for anything. We'll *never* get her out of book club."

Puddin was continuing, smirking, "But you see, the glass paperweight symbolized the beauty of the past and Winston's struggle to understand it."

Blanche asked slowly, "Winston can't understand the past?"

"No!" said Puddin, shaking her head. "Because it was rewritten by the government so much!"

"Oh, she's loving this," muttered Myrtle.

"Then there's them telescreen things. Awful! Them can spy on you *an'* force you to watch that propaganda stuff," said Puddin.

It went on and on with Puddin covering everything that Myrtle and Miles would have brought up during their own turns.

Miles said quietly, "I'll hand it to her—she does have a good memory. She doesn't even have notes in front of her."

"And yet she can't remember when it's her day to clean my house," said Myrtle sourly.

Everyone else's turn was not nearly as good as Puddin's. They just reported their feelings about the book. When Myrtle's turn came up she said shortly, "I have nothing more to add." At this point, Myrtle wanted to get the sharing time over with so that they could listen to Philomena. Hopefully the club members weren't so attuned to propaganda after reading *1984* that they could recognize Philomena's talk for the propaganda it was.

Philomena began slowly, talking about her own life of reading and how much richer it was when she first decided to expand into other genres and then more deeply into classical literature. "It opens up your mind so much."

The club members looked at her doubtfully, unsure whether they wanted their minds opened or not.

Philomena offered ideas for where to go after reading *1984,* and then suggestions following that. She'd carefully created a handout for each member with all of her suggestions and why she thought they might be a good match for the club.

Miles said quietly, "Well, she's done everything she can. I suppose it's up to us now."

Myrtle nodded. She frowned as she saw the ladies' crinkled brows as they surveyed the handout. It didn't look as though they were exactly thrilled by the idea of reading any of them.

Everyone clapped politely however. Myrtle hissed to Miles, "Now remember, I wanted to ask Philomena about what her brother said. That she'd been dating Gabriel."

Miles said, "You really think you're going to have the opportunity to speak with her alone?"

"Why not? Most of the ladies are probably going to avoid talking to her in case she tries to convince them to start on her reading list," said Myrtle.

Sure enough, at the end of the meeting, Philomena was standing awkwardly by herself. Myrtle swooped in. Miles tried swooping too, but he was waylaid by one of the merry widows in the club. He gave Myrtle a miserable look as he was ensnared.

Myrtle said, "You did a wonderful job, Philomena. And I loved that you printed out your suggestions for the group."

Philomena smiled at her but her eyes were doubtful. "Do you think so? I'm not sure—they all seemed a little resistant to the idea."

"They're simply slow to embrace change. I'll be sure to bring up your book list at every opportunity," said Myrtle.

Philomena said politely, "You seem to have a very solid book club. There were certainly a lot of members here for the meeting. I was surprised to see Puddin here, too. I need to ask her how she's enjoying the Sherlock book."

Myrtle pursed her lips together. She'd be shocked indeed if Puddin had made any headway at all with the Sherlock book. She was also dying to note that Puddin's commentary on *1984* was all taken directly from Myrtle's own analyses but realized it would make her sound churlish to say so. Instead she grudgingly said, "Yes, Puddin seems to be engaging in quite the cultural Renaissance lately. I believe she's planning on attending the garden club gala tomorrow, too."

Philomena said, crinkling her brow in thought, "She seems like so much more of a *perceptive* person than I'd have thought, too."

"Yes, doesn't she seem so?" said Myrtle rather flatly.

Philomena said in a hushed voice, "Which is exactly why I thought she might be involved in those murders. She's more than she appears."

"But completely incapable of murder, I assure you," said Myrtle.

Myrtle paused. Then she decided that there was no great segue from book club and garden club to ex-boyfriends, so she simply came out with it. "By the way, I was speaking to your brother yesterday. Such a nice young man."

Philomena smiled. "I'm surprised that you had the opportunity to catch up with him. It seems as though he's always working."

"He was actually coming off of a shift when I was speaking with him," said Myrtle. "And he was still generous enough to make sure that I was all right after I felt faint."

Philomena said proudly, "It sounds like him. Did you have a nice talk?"

"It was brief. Although he did mention something that I found a little confusing. He said that you and Gabriel had been having an affair," said Myrtle.

Philomena's face turned pink and she glanced around quickly to ensure no one was listening in. Myrtle wasn't sure if Philomena's blush was because she'd been caught in a fib or because of shyness related to talking about her personal life.

She said, "We were seeing each other for a little while, yes. He was in an unhappy marriage. It didn't last very long because he called it off." Philomena sighed. "I'm sorry I wasn't more forthright about it, but to be honest, it's something that I try not to think about. It wasn't a happy time for me. And I've kept it very quiet."

Philomena glanced at her watch. "I'm so sorry, Miss Myrtle, but I need to leave for the library. Thanks again for inviting me to speak here. See you at the gala."

Myrtle was going to rescue Miles from his conversation when Tippy walked up to her. She said, "Your friend Puddin is a dark horse! I never would have guessed that she had such a talent for literary analysis."

"Yes, few would guess that," said Myrtle a bit sourly.

"I guess it just goes to show that you can't judge a book by its cover," said Tippy.

Myrtle said, "I suppose not."

"You'll be bringing her back each month, won't you? I really appreciated her insights today on the book. I have to admit that I didn't actually enjoy the story very much, but I gained a whole new perspective after she delved into the symbolism and theme and other aspects of the book," said Tippy.

Georgia was gathering her plate of muffins and interjected, "Bring 'er back! I loved hearing what she said about that book. I was about to apologize for making the club read it until she talked about it a little."

Tippy added in a low voice, "Although I do think it might be a good idea if the club reading list veered off into less-challenging waters. We were really pushing our comprehension level with this one."

Myrtle gritted her teeth, but then managed to say in a somewhat polite tone, "Sometimes you have to push yourself to grow."

Tippy blinked as if growth were the last thing she expected to gain through the book club . . . somewhere behind having a social outlet and networking with others.

Myrtle said, "Thanks for hosting again. I should leave—I'm sure Puddin has things to do."

She looked around for Puddin and saw her surreptitiously wrapping hors d'oeuvres in a napkin. Puddin jumped when Myrtle called her name and then said sourly, "Don't want them goin' to waste."

Myrtle glanced around for Miles and saw him give her a desperate nonverbal plea for help as the conversation he was embroiled in didn't appear to be wrapping up anytime soon.

"Miles," called Myrtle in a peremptory fashion. "Could you drive me back home, now?"

Miles extricated himself from the conversation in great relief. "Coming!"

They walked outside Tippy's house and to Miles's car. "At least that's over," grumbled Myrtle.

Miles asked Puddin with some trepidation, "What did you think of book club now that you've been to a complete meeting?"

Puddin said carelessly, "I dunno. I won't go back, though."

"You won't?" asked Myrtle, a slow smile spreading on her face.

"Nope. Too much work to read them books. And the food weren't so good, neither," said Puddin.

"Although I notice that didn't stop you from taking a good deal of it home," said Myrtle.

Puddin shrugged. "Dusty'll eat anything. Maybe I won't need to cook tonight now."

"And I suppose you won't have to cook anything tomorrow night if you bring food back from the gala," said Myrtle with a roll of her eyes.

Miles cleared his throat. "As a matter of interest, Puddin, what were you planning on wearing to the gala?"

Puddin stuck her chin up in the air although the folks in the front seat couldn't see it. "Ain't what I got on okay?"

Myrtle said, "Black pants and a black shirt go lots of places, but at the gala, someone may think you're part of the wait staff. Do you have a scarf you could pair with it, maybe?"

Puddin made a face. "Too hot to wear a scarf, Miss Myrtle!"

"I don't mean a *winter* scarf. I mean a decorative scarf," said Myrtle.

Puddin considered this for a couple of seconds. "Nope."

"Well, I have one that you're welcome to borrow," said Myrtle with a shrug.

Puddin was quiet for a few moments in the backseat. Then she muttered something under her breath.

"What was that?" asked Myrtle sharply.

"I just said that I'm not your same age. Maybe the scarf thing won't look good on me as on you," said Puddin.

Miles smiled at Puddin's attempt at diplomacy. He pointed out, "Not that I have any desire to go there, but we are approaching the Centerville Dress Shop."

Myrtle brightened. "That's perfect. Puddin can buy a scarf and we can speak with Alice Porper again."

Puddin said, "Puddin ain't buying nothing. I'm broke, remember? And still haven't got my money from Mr. Subers."

"But Alice Porper is the person that he left all of his money to, Puddin. So if you have any hope of getting that money you're owed back, you might as well bring it up with her. But let's handle the topic carefully and *after* I've asked her a couple of questions," said Myrtle as Miles pulled off the road and into the shop's parking lot.

Puddin grumbled, "Seems she'd be buttered up enough by us buying stuff."

"Regardless, we're not here to pressure her," said Myrtle sternly as she and Puddin got out of the car. "Coming, Miles?"

"Not this time. I've read all the magazines of interest. I'll stay in the car. Take your time," said Miles. He was putting his seat back down as if preparing for a nap.

Puddin screwed up her face in thought as she and Myrtle walked toward the store. "Alice Porper. Right. So her is that woman with Mr. Subers."

Myrtle said, "She's the woman that you recognized leaving Amos Subers house. Or perhaps the woman that you hallucinated leaving there since she spends almost all her time at the dress shop."

"Probably'll spend less time now she got money," prophesized Puddin.

Chapter Nineteen

The bell rang as they entered and Alice, wearing a bright blue dress and her hair swinging loose on her shoulders, looked up from behind the checkout counter. She gave Myrtle a genuine smile as she stood up. "Miss Myrtle! How did the outfit work out?"

"It was perfect," said Myrtle, returning the smile. "And now I'm back, but with Puddin."

Alice put her hand out and Puddin reluctantly shook it as if shaking hands was a foreign and rather invasive experience. "It's good to meet you, Puddin."

"She's going to the gala tomorrow and needs a scarf to wear with the outfit she's wearing now," said Myrtle.

Alice gave Puddin's black top and black pants a quick and experienced appraisal. She strode over to a table that had a variety of different accessories on it. After a few moments of careful thought, she pulled out a colorful red print. "Try this one," she said, handing it to Puddin.

Puddin handled the scarf as though it were a poisonous snake. Myrtle sighed.

Alice said, "May I?" She positioned Puddin in front of a nearby mirror and tied the scarf around her neck. "There. What do you think?"

Puddin preened. "Looks good."

"I thought a colorful scarf for a colorful personality would work well," said Alice with a smile.

Myrtle suddenly remembered the tickets still burning a hole in her purse. Red had paid for the remainder of them, but if she sold one, she'd make a profit. "Speaking of the gala, are you at all interested in gardening, Alice?"

Alice laughed. "Before you go any further, you should know that Tippy Chambers has already beaten you to it. She sold me gala tickets weeks ago."

Myrtle grimaced. "I should have known. Tippy has been a ticket-selling whiz kid. And naturally, she probably spends a good deal of time here." And money.

Alice said, "She seems thrilled about the event. Her excitement was contagious." She smiled at Myrtle. "I suppose you'll be going with your young man?"

Myrtle's eyes widened. "Pardon?"

"I mean Miles. Everyone is always so jealous of the amount of time the two of you spend together," said Alice with a grin.

Puddin snickered, her eyes full of malicious merriment.

Myrtle said with a hint of frost in her voice, "Then everyone is very silly. Miles is far too young for me. Besides, we're friends."

Alice beamed at her. "That's the best type of relationship."

"Alas, I'm attending the gala with Puddin and my friend Wanda," said Myrtle with a tight smile. "Although Miles will certainly be there." She paused. She had fewer misgivings about probing into Alice's personal life since she'd just probed into her own.

Myrtle jumped right in. "I was actually wondering how much longer you might be working here or if you'll be putting in as many hours as you were. I would miss getting your help here if so."

Alice flushed. "I suppose people are talking about it all over town. I was as surprised as anyone when the lawyer told me that I was inheriting Amos's estate. Of course, I haven't gotten a penny of it yet. It all makes me feel sort of sick, to tell you the truth."

Puddin made a scoffing noise and Myrtle gave her a repressing look. "How do you mean?"

Alice said sadly, "Oh, I don't know. I suppose because at the time Amos made the will, he clearly thought that we had some sort of future together. But then he deliberately did things to sabotage our relationship. It didn't make any sense."

Myrtle said, "What did you think about how he left his daughter out of the will?"

Puddin made clucking noises at this and Myrtle gave her a discreet kick until she stopped.

Alice's face was sober. "It was a shock. It's as though he wrote his will specifically to hurt Josephine. I never was much of a fan of Josephine, but I'll say one thing for her: she was devoted to her father. Once everything settles down and I actually receive Amos's estate, I'll have to make sure to provide for his daughter. It's only right."

Puddin gave Myrtle a prompting look. Myrtle cleared her throat and said, "On that note, Alice, Puddin here was also wondering if you could possibly pay her monies owed by Amos when the estate settles."

Alice smiled at Puddin. "Of course I will. I could write you a check right now, if it's not too much." She shook her head. "Isn't that just like Amos? A cheapskate to the end."

Puddin exclaimed, "Fifty dollars!" and then anxiously watched to see if Alice thought that amount too great to reach for a checkbook.

But Alice immediately wrote Puddin a check for the amount. "I'm sorry that Amos treated you like that. It must have made you very frustrated."

Puddin took the check from her. "But I didn't kill 'im!"

"Of course not," said Alice soothingly.

Myrtle said to Alice, "You must feel as though your head is spinning. It's been quite a week, hasn't it?"

Puddin, bored now that her check was in her pocket, took a stroll around the store.

Alice nodded. "Yes. And I was so shocked to hear about Gabriel as well. We'd only just seen him at Amos's funeral that morning."

Myrtle said, "There had been talk that Gabriel might have been blackmailing someone over Amos's death. That perhaps he knew something."

Puddin exclaimed over one of the price tags and hastily put the garment back on the rack as if she might have to pay for it for looking at it.

Alice frowned, tilting her head to one side. "Blackmail doesn't really sound like Gabriel."

"Doesn't it?" asked Myrtle.

"No. Don't get me wrong—he was no angel and had a devilish sense of humor. But I don't see him profiting off Amos's death. Although I *can* see him telling the person that he knew what had happened. He liked to hold things over people's heads," said Alice.

"Did you like him?" asked Myrtle.

Alice gave a short laugh. "I liked that Amos and he got along so well. But there was a little tension between us. Sometimes I think Gabriel was a little jealous over how close Amos and I were at one point. He would ask to go to the movies with us or to a concert and groups of three usually don't work as well—somebody always gets left out. And Gabriel's wife has never been one to enjoy going out."

Myrtle said, "Who do you think could be responsible for Gabriel's death?"

Alice sighed. "I really don't know. Although after the funeral, I was in the parking lot and heard Josephine and Gabriel having an argument."

Myrtle raised her eyebrows. "At the cemetery? How remarkable. What was the argument about?"

"I didn't hear all of it because I didn't want to seem to be snooping. But Gabriel seemed to be telling Josephine not to count her chickens before they hatched or some such." Alice gave a shrug.

"What do you think he meant by that?" asked Myrtle. "And what did Josephine say?"

Alice said, "I really didn't have any idea until the lawyer spoke with me. Then I guessed that perhaps Gabriel already knew about Amos's will and was trying to give Josephine a hint that she might not be inheriting his estate."

"Which probably made her furious," said Myrtle thoughtfully.

Alice said dryly, "Josephine did tell him to drop dead." Then she covered her mouth with her hands and her eyes grew wide.

"No one is fond of the bearer of bad news," said Myrtle.

Alice said in a horrified voice, "But surely Josephine wouldn't have *murdered* Gabriel because she was angry about him hinting about the inheritance?"

Myrtle shook her head. "Not likely. But what if Gabriel also used that opportunity to tell her to meet him later at his garage? That he had seen or knew something?"

Alice put her hand up to her neck. "Mercy. That's truly awful. I never really thought that I could feel sorry for Gabriel, but now I can't seem to help myself."

Puddin was now suspiciously surveying the shop's lingerie collection.

"Could you see Josephine reacting like that?" asked Myrtle. "I don't know her very well."

Alice thought about this for a minute. "As much as I hate to say it, I think I could. She has a good self-preservation instinct. And she's tough as nails. I don't believe that she was ever crazy about Gabriel, either. She thought he was a bad influence on her father." She paused and said as Puddin wandered back over to them, "You know, we have a pair of earrings that would go really well with the new scarf."

Puddin shot Myrtle a sideways glance.

Myrtle shook her head quickly. "We're done for today, but thanks. Did you ever tell me whether you were planning on remaining at the shop?"

Alice laughed. "I can tell that you are a natural-born reporter, Miss Myrtle. The truth is that I really don't know. I know I won't put in as many hours as I do now, for sure. But I might be bored if I completely retired. It's good to stay busy, isn't it?"

Myrtle totally agreed. That was not to say that one of the highlights of her day wasn't watching her soap opera, but she couldn't imagine spending the rest of it hanging around the house.

"See you at the gala!" called Alice as Myrtle and Puddin walked to the door.

Suddenly Myrtle snapped her fingers. "Forgot something!"

"The earrings?" asked Puddin hopefully.

"No, poor Wanda," said Myrtle. She turned around. "Alice, I should probably pick up a top or something for my other friend who is going to the gala." Myrtle frowned as she tried to remember exactly what her bank balance was. Then she smiled as she remembered that Miles had offered to pay. "Puddin, if you could run out and ask Miles for his credit card?"

Alice, who worked on commission, beamed at her. "Of course, Miss Myrtle. What size is your friend?"

"Triple zero," muttered Puddin, walking out, with the derisive snort of someone who had never been a triple zero.

"She's very thin. Too thin. Maybe if you have something that covers that up? And maybe something that isn't too expensive?" Myrtle wasn't sure of the exact extent of Miles's generosity and was still reflecting on the nebulous nature of her own bank account.

Alice said in a swift, understanding fashion, "We do have an excellent selection on the clearance rack."

Myrtle suddenly felt more cheerful. "Yes, I'm sure you do."

Puddin walked back in and presented Myrtle with the card.

Alice strode over to the clearance rack. "What color should I try to match with?" asked Alice, giving the rack a calculating look.

"Black," said Myrtle and Puddin in chorus.

A few minutes later, Myrtle and Puddin were getting back into Miles's car. As Myrtle suspected, he was sound asleep. He woke with a start when they slammed the car doors.

He readjusted his seat and rubbed his eyes. "We're all good?"

Puddin apparently didn't seem to think so. "Except I gotta go to the gala with a witch."

"You should be happy that you're going at all and with a new scarf, to boot," snapped Myrtle. "You're not even interested in gardening like Wanda is. You're just there to eat free food and bring a plate home to Dusty."

"Ain't nuthin' wrong with that! Leastways I'm honest about it. Why does the witch suddenly wanna garden? For food? Guess the witchin' business ain't been so good lately," said Puddin with a shrug.

Myrtle rolled her eyes. "*Anyway*, I picked up a new top for Wanda with your card. I'll put the receipt in your wallet."

"Are we taking it to her now?" asked Miles.

"No, I'll tell her we'll pick her up early tomorrow so that she can come to my house and change," said Myrtle.

"If her house phone is all paid up," said Miles.

Myrtle said, "She has that phone that Sloan gave her for newspaper business. I'll call her on that."

Miles said, "So what time tomorrow, then? Seven? And what are our plans between now and then?"

Myrtle said, "Seven works. And my plan involves writing another article for Sloan and then doing some thinking. I feel as though I should know something. But I don't know what it is."

Puddin said, "I'm just glad I got my fifty dollars."

"All in all, I'm really tired of hearing about that money, Puddin," said Myrtle in a warning tone. "Although it was sweet of Alice to give it to you."

Puddin nodded, looking lazily out of the car window. "And now she's rolling in it. Lotsa money."

Myrtle said, "She's nice to want to give something to Josephine, considering the two of them never really got along."

"It's only fair," said Puddin. Then she glanced at Myrtle, "What are *you* wearin' to the gala?"

"Me? I haven't even spared it a thought. I'll simply pull some black slacks and a white or yellow blouse out of the closet and pair it with some pearls and black shoes. It's easy enough," said Myrtle.

"No one is asking what *I'm* wearing to the gala," observed Miles mildly.

"No one is asking because everyone knows what you'll wear," said Myrtle. "It'll either be the gray suit with the red tie—"

"Or them khakis an' blue sportscoat," said Puddin, finishing up.

"Am I that predictable?" asked Miles with a grimace as he pulled the car into Puddin's driveway.

"In a good way," assured Myrtle.

Puddin grinned in the backseat.

The next evening Miles picked Wanda up early to drop her off at Myrtle's house to get ready. He muttered to Myrtle, "You may want to feed her a little, too. Otherwise, you know what may happen."

"Otherwise she might eat most of the food at the gala," said Myrtle. "Got it. Although I haven't run an inventory of my pantry yet. Red might have had a couple more meals out of me."

Miles left to get changed before he picked up Puddin. Then he would drive all four of them to the gala.

Myrtle said to Wanda, "I hope you'll like this top I found for you. I figured it would go well with your black pants." Not that Wanda ever wore any other color of pant. For all Myrtle knew, it was the same pair each time.

She removed the garment bag and presented the top to Wanda. Myrtle was a little nervous about the top. The reason it might have been on the clearance rack was likely because it was a bit too sparkly for the average Bradley matron. It was red with black sequins and an asymmetric hem with a fringe hem sleeve that would reach Wanda's elbows.

Wanda reached out and touched the top reverently before taking it gently from Myrtle. She looked solemnly at Myrtle. "Thank you. And Miles, too."

"You're very welcome Wanda, but I only hope it fits! It was the smallest size the shop carried," said Myrtle. "Try it on and then we'll eat a snack before the event."

Wanda shook her head, carefully touching a sequin. "Better eat now and try it on after. Don't wanna spill on it."

"Good point," said Myrtle. She frowned. "Oh wait. Speaking of spills, I just remembered that I spilled mayo on my new funeral outfit after Amos's service. It's still at the cleaners."

"Got other clothes?" asked Wanda, walking toward the kitchen.

"That's an excellent question. Ordinarily the answer would be yes, but I have the feeling that the dry cleaner is actually the repository of more than one outfit," said Myrtle, frowning even more ferociously.

She hurried to the kitchen and yanked open the pantry. "I'll pull out some ideas for things for you to eat, Wanda, and then I better see what I can find to wear." Myrtle hurriedly pulled out cereal, milk, bread, ham, cheese, tomatoes, and chips and then strode off to her room.

When she opened the closet, she groaned. "This isn't good," she muttered, sliding the hangers around and looking at the clothes. Nothing said *gala*. Many of the choices didn't even say *Bo's Diner*. She made a face.

Wanda wandered in, holding a sandwich and surveying her closet thoughtfully.

"What do you think, Wanda?" asked Myrtle.

"I think you should git to the dry cleaner," said Wanda.

"It's too late. They close at noon on Saturdays and it's far past that, anyway," said Myrtle.

Wanda tilted her head to one side and then pointed to a pair of polyester gabardine pull-on slacks and a turquoise poly knit top with a banded bottom.

"Really? I don't think one wears elastic waists at galas," said Myrtle doubtfully. "And I'm not sure about the top either. It blouses out so. Really, the whole ensemble isn't good."

"Beggars can't be choosers," said Wanda.

"I suppose I can dress it up with jewelry," said Myrtle. Although she didn't have the type of jewelry that could dress it up to the extent that was required.

A few minutes later, she walked out to the living room wearing the rather casual ensemble. She found Wanda wearing the new top and admiring herself in the mirror near the front door. Wanda started and blushed.

"That top looks stunning on you, Wanda!" said Myrtle warmly. "Between you and Puddin, I'm going to look vastly underdressed."

"Thanks," muttered Wanda a little shyly. Then, "He's pullin' in the driveway."

A moment later there was a toot of the horn to prove her right. They walked outside to see Puddin, beaming from the front seat.

Chapter Twenty

Miles rolled down his window. "Do you . . . well, will you have trouble getting in and out of the backseat, Myrtle?" He gave Myrtle's ensemble a confused stare.

"Certainly not! I'm fine sitting in the backseat with Wanda." Myrtle devoutly hoped that no one was actually paying any attention to the length of time that it took her to fold her legs into the car. She blamed it all on the fact that she had to put the blasted cane in first.

Puddin was pleased as punch at being in the front seat with Miles, but her eyes darkened as Wanda quietly climbed in next to Myrtle. She started muttering what sounded like dire statements under her breath as Miles pulled out of the driveway and headed out toward the Bradley Country Club.

Myrtle ignored her. "So tell me, Wanda, what are you looking forward to tonight? And how is your gardening going?" She smiled. "Sort of like the old nursery rhyme: *how does your garden grow*?"

Wanda said solemnly, "Garden is okay. Tomatoes ain't so hot. Lookin' forward to the guy talking about herbs." She paused. "An' keepin' Puddin safe."

Puddin exploded from the front seat. "Just you keep yerself safe! Never needed nobody to protect me."

Miles sighed at the inauspicious start to the evening.

Myrtle barked in her schoolteacher voice, "Puddin, declare a truce! Right now. Wanda is trying to be nice."

Puddin pouted but grouched, "Okay." She paused. "I know you just wanna look out for me."

Myrtle said through gritted teeth, "Thank you. Changing the subject, Puddin, what are *you* looking forward to tonight?"

"The chicken pasta," said Puddin with anticipation.

"Besides the food," said Myrtle impatiently.

Puddin drew a blank. "Meetin' people?" she said in an uncertain voice. Then she shrugged.

Fortunately, the trip to the country club didn't take long. This club had been around for ages and was certainly not in the crowning glory it was when Myrtle was a little girl. The golf course was challenging mainly because of the shape the greens were in. The swimming pool was outdated and tufts of grass impudently pushed through cracks in the concrete surrounding it. The clubhouse itself looked rather tired and was in dire need of a fresh coat of white paint and black for the shutters. But it was the only place in town with an outdoor area large enough to hold this sort of event. White tents scattered the grounds. There was a large tent with chairs for the series of speakers and a couple of smaller tents with tables for food. There was even a tent set up for a botanical plant sale (with lots of plastic to keep everyone's fine clothes clean).

They got out of the car. Puddin gaped. "Everybody looks pretty."

"Well, they look their best, anyway." Myrtle sighed as she looked down at her own attire. "All right, let's make plans to meet up at the car at . . . what time, Miles? Ten o'clock? Ten-thirty?"

Puddin and Wanda looked at each other and then lifted up their watch-less arms.

Miles said, "You could both check your phones for the time."

Puddin and Wanda looked at each other again.

"Will we *ever* be able to meet up?" asked Miles, looking discouraged. "Or will we end up camping out at the country club all night?"

Myrtle said, "There aren't enough people in Bradley for us to get *that* separated from each other. I guess let's meet at the car when the last speaker has finished." She tilted her head to one side. "Puddin, this is the first chance I've had to really see that scarf. It looks good on you with the black outfit."

Puddin grinned at her. "Thanks. Might hafta go back there now I got my fifty dollars. Nice of her. Specially since I ain't never laid eyes on her before." She spotted the food tent and said, "Gotta go."

"Hold on!" said Myrtle, but the DJ turned the music volume higher and Myrtle's words were lost.

Wanda said something quietly to Miles and then loped off.

Myrtle said curiously to Miles, "What was Wanda saying to you?"

Miles sighed. "She was pointedly reminding me that ginger ale was good for migraines. I certainly hope that doesn't mean that she foresees a resurgence of my headache."

Myrtle nodded distractedly. "I'll need to talk to Puddin again."

Miles said "I suppose there are a lot of people to talk to tonight. Are we following up with Philomena and/or Alice? Any other suspects here tonight?"

Myrtle gazed over at the ambulance parked some distance from the event and the EMTs standing casually outside it. "Not that he's a suspect, but it looks like Philomena's brother Steven is working the event."

Miles raised his eyebrows. "Is there much need for an ambulance at a garden club gala? Might someone have a coronary at the excitement of learning more about the care of azalea bushes?"

Myrtle said, "More likely that someone faints from the heat. Or, in this town, that someone is a target of a murderer."

"What do you make of Wanda's determination to keep an eye on Puddin?" asked Miles.

Myrtle said, "If I didn't know better, I'd think she was bent on bothering Puddin. But knowing Wanda, I have to assume that she is simply concerned about her safety. And I'm enjoying that *for once*, I'm not the one who's supposed to be in danger."

They walked toward the tents and Miles said, "Isn't that Josephine up there?"

"Josephine? At the garden club gala?" scoffed Myrtle.

"Well, Wanda and Puddin are here. Why not Josephine?" said Miles mildly.

Myrtle squinted ahead. "I don't think Josephine is all that interested in horticulture. Even if she was, there's probably a limited amount she could do while living in an apartment. Oh, wait. I see. It looks as though she's working. She's helping the catering crew and busing tables and whatnot."

Miles said in an undertone, "Sounds like the perfect set-up for murder."

Myrtle said, "Uh-oh. Tippy is heading this way." She fruitlessly searched for a hiding place as the president of the garden club headed her way.

Tippy called out, "Myrtle? Is that you?"

Myrtle grimaced. "Hi, Tippy. Looks like a great event."

Tippy said, "I've heard some great feedback already." She paused and glanced at Myrtle's outfit. "I knew I should have listed the attire on the invitation."

Myrtle didn't defend her clothing. Age had its privileges.

"If you have any extra time tonight, I'd love another volunteer for the golf cart shifts," said Tippy. "It's easy. If you know how to drive a car, you'll have no problem with a golf cart." She frowned. "You do know how to drive a car still, don't you?"

"I drove just the other day," said Myrtle with a sniff. She carefully didn't mention the fact that Miles had found fault with her driving.

"Great! Then you'll have no trouble. We're simply picking up the elderly and infirm and transporting them to their car. You might need a ride yourself, I'd imagine," said Tippy thoughtfully.

"Certainly not!" said Myrtle.

Tippy said in a hurry, "No, I suppose not. By the way, do you have the money for the rest of your tickets?"

Myrtle said, "I didn't want to carry that much cash with me tonight. I'll mail you a check."

"Then you *did* sell the rest of your tickets. Good job, Myrtle, I knew I could count on you," said Tippy, beaming.

Myrtle shifted uncomfortably. "Yes, well, I always like to do what's expected of me. See you later, Tippy."

As they walked away, Miles murmured, "Were you *trying* to be a rebel, or does it come naturally?"

"Don't be silly," said Myrtle, annoyed. "I'm simply forgetful. All of my good clothes are at the dry cleaner. It doesn't even matter since I'm so much more comfortable in what I'm wearing. It was the smartest choice."

Miles said, "What do we do first?"

"Let's get a plate of food and a glass of wine and have a seat," said Myrtle.

"Was wine included in the price of the ticket?" asked Miles, raising his eyebrows.

"Yes, but only the one glass." As a particularly raucous laugh came from a nearby tent Myrtle said, "Of course, it's a cash bar after that."

Miles said, "I'll skip the wine, anyway. Not only am I the driver, but I still have that migraine hovering in the background."

They stood in a particularly long food line. Puddin, Myrtle noticed, was much nearer the front. Either a rush of people had gotten in the line after Puddin, or else she had cut in front of everyone. Myrtle rather suspected the latter. Myrtle tried calling out to her, but she either couldn't hear her or deliberately ignored her.

Maisy Perry walked toward them with a smile. "Miles! Just the person that I wanted to see."

Miles flinched, knowing that this couldn't portend anything good. "Hello, Maisy," he said warily.

Another loud burst of raucous laughter from the table of revelers made Maisy jump. Myrtle sighed. Maisy was the poster child for nervousness. Her thin body trembled at the smallest provocation and her wide gaze from behind her huge glasses seemed to have a horrified expression all the time. Myrtle usually ended conversations with Maisy feeling anxious, herself as if it were some horrid, communicable condition.

Maisy said to Miles, "I was hoping you might be interested in joining a Scrabble club that my friends and I are putting together." She glanced over at Myrtle and said reluctantly, "You too, Myrtle, of course."

Miles gave a short laugh. "I wouldn't advise bringing Myrtle in unless it's an advanced group. And I'm honored, Maisy, but I don't think I have time in my schedule for playing Scrabble on a competitive basis."

"Oh, it's simply games among friends," pressed Maisy. "At the *church*, so you know it can't be too cutthroat." She gave a tinkling laugh.

Miles looked desperately at Myrtle for some sort of escape route. Myrtle shrugged. They couldn't get out of the food line if they wanted to eat, and Maisy was sure to continue extolling the virtues of the club the entire time. Myrtle didn't particularly want to hear Maisy get whiny, so she threw Miles a lifeline.

"As a matter of fact, Maisy, Miles has been taking a class and doesn't have much free time at all," said Myrtle breezily.

Miles nodded eagerly in agreement.

Maisy asked Miles earnestly, "What type of class and when does it meet? Maybe there wouldn't be a conflict."

Miles looked to Myrtle for rescuing as he drew a blank as to what type of class he was taking.

"An art class. When does the Scrabble club meet?" asked Myrtle.

"Saturdays at noon."

"Pity. That's precisely when his art class meets. Isn't that right, Miles?" asked Myrtle.

Maisy's face fell and then she said in a chipper voice, "Well, the nice thing about being a club president is that I have the leeway to change the meeting time! I'll change it if you'll come, Miles."

Miles looked down into Maisy's anxious face. He reluctantly said, "All right."

Maisy clapped her hands. As they ambled toward the food, she regaled Miles with the general wonderfulness of the group, the space, the sense of respect between players, and how well he was going to fit in while he glumly proceeded through the line.

Then, Myrtle and Miles were both aghast as Erma Sherman sat down at their table. "How's the case going?" she demanded in a voice that was far too loud.

The only good thing about seeing Erma, reflected Myrtle, was that it made her feel better about what she was wearing. "It's fine," she answered in the kind of tone that indicated it was the end of the conversation.

Erma next turned her vile attentions on Miles. "Good to see you here at the gala. You really should join garden club."

Miles looked distressed at this further assault on his free time. "No time," he muttered desperately.

Erma said, pursing her lips, "Well, that *is* a shame. Because you've got crabgrass in your yard and I'd think you'd be looking for some help in getting rid of it."

Myrtle glared at Erma. "If Miles has crabgrass in his yard, it's because it's been infested by *your* yard, Erma. As you very well know."

Erma gave her braying laugh and said, "Anyway, think about it. Boy, am I glad I made it tonight. I've had the worst intestinal problems this past week."

Myrtle and Miles grimaced as Erma droned on about a most inappropriate topic over dinner. When she finally stopped short, they blinked in surprise.

Erma was gaping across the tent. "Why, *Wanda* is here!" She gave Myrtle an accusatory stare. "You didn't tell me that Wanda was going to be here."

"Should I have?" asked Myrtle, still annoyed at sitting next to Erma at all.

"Of course! I'm a huge fan of hers. Remember when I asked you to tell me the next time she was over at your house? But I've not heard from you about her," said Erma.

Myrtle gave her a tight smile.

Miles, his curiosity forcing him to break his traditional silence when it came to Erma, said, "And why are you a fan of Wanda's?"

Erma said, "Don't you read the paper? She wrote a horoscope a few weeks ago that said *Erma, call the electrician.*"

"Did you call him?" asked Miles.

"Did I call him? Of *course* I called him! If a psychic calls me out by name and tells me to call an electrician, I'll do exactly what she says. And guess what?" asked Erma.

Myrtle and Miles waited, but naturally Erma was one of those annoying people that actually made you *ask*. "What?" they both said impatiently.

"When he got to my house, he found a wiring hazard that could have burned down my house! Burned the whole thing down! What's more, it was during that windy period—maybe it could have burned down *your* house, too, Miles!" Erma's eyes gleamed at the thought of the potential carnage.

Wanda walked up to them. She did not seem to have made it to the food yet and she eyed the spread hungrily. Then she said to Miles, "You goin' to listen to the next lecture?"

Miles looked confused and Myrtle said, "*I'm* listening to the next lecture."

Wanda shook her head and Myrtle shrugged. "Well, I was planning on it, anyway," she said.

Miles said, "I suppose I could listen to it. What's the program on?"

"The Many Uses of Herbs," said Wanda. "Could you record it for me? Does your phone do that?"

Miles said, "It does. Although I admit that I don't have much cause to use the function." He frowned. "Can't you make the lecture?"

Wanda shook her head. "Got to watch Puddin."

Miles absently rubbed at his temple with a hand. Wanda added pointedly, "Should git yerself some ginger for that."

Erma, who was wriggling with excitement finally couldn't contain herself any more. "Wanda, I wanted to let you know that I'm a huge fan of yours! And thanks for that tip on the electrician. Boy, that was right on the mark."

Wanda, who appeared distracted and kept scanning the crowd, grunted in indication that she heard Erma.

Erma said, "In fact, I wondered if you might to go on a little trip with me. Sometimes I take these jaunts to Mississippi and do some light gambling. You might be useful to have along." Erma gave one of her big grins, exposing her large front teeth.

"Gotta go," muttered Wanda.

Erma said, "At least take a picture with me! Miles can take it for us. You're my hero!"

Wanda gave Erma a considering look, then leaned forward and muttered something quietly to her. And then Wanda hurried off into the crowd.

Erma said, "A selfie with Wanda! She's set it all up for me." She glanced at her watch and abruptly heaved herself from her chair and rushed away to torment other victims.

Chapter Twenty-One

Myrtle slumped in relief. "That must have been a record for an Erma encounter."

"Well, we couldn't exactly get up and move to another seat," said Miles, rubbing his temples. He gazed at the people walking past the tent. "Looks like Sloan did take your advice and bring Sally here on a date." He paused. "I can't say it's the most *thrilling* of dates, though. And it looks as though he might even be working. He sure is taking a lot of pictures, if not."

"It's a better date than discussing the updates for the newspaper website," said Myrtle. She peered across the tent. "It looks as if Josephine is taking a break. This might be a good time to go talk with her." She then frowned as she surveyed the food line. "But there's Alice Porper. It might be good to talk with her, too."

Miles said, "Isn't that the benefit of having two of us here? We can split up." He looked especially pleased with himself for the idea.

Myrtle considered this. "You don't ever speak to suspects one-on-one, though."

Miles said with dignity, "Only because I don't have the opportunity."

Myrtle tilted her head to one side, thoughtfully. "The only problem with that is that Alice is an unattached female of a certain age. You might blind her with your aura of distinguished attractiveness and make her stammer."

"All the better to catch her off-guard," said Miles.

Myrtle said, "Or I could send you to talk to Josephine. She's likely too young for you to set her heart aflutter."

"Thanks," said Miles, making a face.

"All right, I'm decided. You speak to Josephine and I'll speak to Alice. We're just talking about the event and then seeing if they've remembered anything else that might be helpful regarding either Amos's or Gabriel's death," said Myrtle. "Try to stay focused."

Miles said with a shrug, "Josephine has already disappeared while we were talking. And, now that I glance at my watch and my program, I see that it's time for Wanda's lecture."

"You could *always* skip it. They'll stream it online later," said Myrtle.

Miles raised his eyebrows. "And Wanda would watch that . . . how?"

It was true. Wanda wasn't exactly set-up for technology at the hubcap shack. Myrtle sighed. "All right, then. I'll go speak with Alice and you go tape Wanda's lecture."

Miles reached in his jacket pocket for his phone and then frowned. He pulled out a small piece of paper. "What's this?"

Myrtle peered at it. "Considering the chicken-scratch, it must be a note from Wanda."

"How on earth am I supposed to read it?" asked Miles. He turned it from side to side and then upside-down.

"Here, give it to me," said Myrtle impatiently, pulling it from his hand. "For heaven's sake. Alice is likely to disappear in the interim." She studied the paper for a few seconds. "It says for you to remember the ginger ale for your headache."

Miles said, "This must be the second or third time I've heard this from her. And I don't even have a headache."

"It sounds as if she's keeping an eye on you and your headache as well as Puddin's safety. She'll be exhausted by the end of the evening," said Myrtle.

Miles glanced at his watch and said, "I need to get going to that lecture."

Myrtle said, "I'm going to try to talk to Alice. And I need to talk to Puddin if I see her. See you later."

Miles walked toward the lecture tent and then turned around, the faintest of headaches starting up. "Myrtle! Do you still have the ginger ale?"

But his voice was swallowed up by the crowd and the music as Myrtle continued walking away.

Myrtle was having no luck spotting Alice, Philomena, or Josephine. She felt as though she had walked for hours. It was as if they were trying to be deliberate impediments. Instead, she'd kept running into people that she'd rather not talk to and would prefer to avoid. What's more, her feet were starting to hurt from walking on the parking lot asphalt.

There was a jaunty honk of a horn and Myrtle looked behind her to see Tippy smiling at her from the golf cart. "Would you like that ride now, Myrtle?"

Myrtle was about to snap a rejection but then hesitated. "What time is it, Tippy?"

Tippy glanced at her diamond dinner watch. "Nearly nine, why?"

Myrtle gave her a sweet smile. "I'd like to take a turn on the golf cart." It was getting late, and this may be her only opportunity to speak to all of the people she wanted to.

Tippy brightened. "Really? Why, that would be absolutely wonderful Myrtle, if you don't mind. I haven't had the chance to attend any of the lectures so far and there's one coming up that I particularly wanted to listen to."

Myrtle said, "I'm happy to give our seniors a spin for a while. *Now*." This because Tippy didn't seem to be in any hurry to dismount.

Tippy then carefully dismounted and said. "You do know how to drive it?"

"Naturally," said Myrtle.

"All right then. If you have any trouble or if you want to be relieved of your duty, just call me," said Tippy.

Myrtle carefully climbed into the driver's seat and gave Tippy an impatient wave. She lurched off with Tippy frowning after her.

After a few minutes, Myrtle concluded that driving a golf cart was most certainly *not* like driving a car. Whoever had come up with such a ridiculous notion was clearly demented. Her driving was wild, her braking jerky.

Myrtle scanned the crowd for Alice, Josephine, or Philomena. The entire town seemed to be at the gala. It was no wonder she had such a hard time selling her tickets. An elderly man with a walking stick waved her down for a ride. "You walk better than I do!" snapped Myrtle as she drove on. The man shook his walking stick at her. She proceeded to turn down four more requests for rides.

"I'm telling Tippy!" called out Tessa McLendon angrily behind her as Myrtle sped away.

She briefly saw Miles waving at her from some distance away and shook her head impatiently. "Can't stop now!" she mouthed.

A minute later, Myrtle spotted a lean figure in front of the swimming pool gate. Wanda. She parked the golf cart and grabbed her cane, leaving her purse in the cart. "Where's Puddin?" she asked.

Wanda said to Myrtle, "You and I are walkin.'"

Myrtle followed Wanda as she pushed open the old metal gate leading to the pool.

"That should be locked," said Myrtle with a frown.

"Anything else botherin' you?" asked Wanda.

Myrtle said, "What, about the case? As a matter of fact, there is. Puddin said that she'd never even seen Alice Porper. Not that Puddin realized this was an important clue, of course. So who *did* Puddin see leaving Amos's house the morning of his murder?"

Wanda raised an eyebrow.

"I bet you have a pretty good idea, being a psychic and all. But I've pieced it together, too. Puddin must have gotten Amos's girlfriends confused. If it wasn't Alice, it must have been Philomena," said Myrtle.

Wanda opened a door into the pool house.

"Everything here is shockingly unlocked," muttered Myrtle again. "Anyway, you must be following Puddin because Philomena is onto her."

"Why is Philomena after her?" drawled Wanda in the tone of someone who already knows.

"Because Puddin is such a big mouth," said Myrtle with a sigh. "She bragged about knowing who the killer was and then told her gossipy cousin. What's more, Puddin was at the garage when Gabriel was discovered. She might have seen or heard something that she realized later pointed to Philomena."

"But you ain't lookin' fer Philomena. Yer lookin' fer Puddin," noted Wanda.

"Because Puddin is hopelessly inept at staying out of trouble. I don't want anything to happen to her," said Myrtle grudgingly.

Wanda peered through the window of the clubhouse out to the pool deck outside. "Found you both of 'em," she said in a serious voice.

Myrtle took a quick look through the window. Puddin was sitting on a chaise by the pool, eating. Myrtle watched in horror as Philomena slipped up behind Puddin and put her hands around Puddin's neck.

Myrtle plowed through the door, brandishing her cane. "Stop that!" she bellowed in a commanding teacher's voice.

Philomena turned around in shock and moved threateningly toward Myrtle.

"Leave her alone," said Puddin furiously.

Philomena snorted. "As if you two could stop anybody."

Wanda walked out the door staring levelly at Philomena. Just her appearance was enough to make Philomena stop in her tracks. Then she rushed to the clubhouse door, shoving Wanda aside to get in.

Wanda raised her voice. "Miles and Erma! She's comin'!"

Myrtle frowned. Miles and Erma?

Myrtle and Puddin hurried through the clubhouse behind Wanda. Miles shook a broken ginger ale bottle at Philomena on one side and Erma menacingly swung a shovel at her on the other.

But they underestimated Philomena's determination to get away. She wheeled wildly around to run. Which was when Tippy hit her with the golf cart, knocking her flat.

Myrtle stood over Philomena, holding her cane threateningly. When Philomena didn't stir, Myrtle said briskly, "Miles, call Red for me."

Tippy, her face white, shakily hopped out of the golf cart. "Oh no," she gasped, looking at Philomena lying prostrate on the ground. "I was looking for you, Myrtle, to find out why you weren't on your golf cart shift. I'd heard allegations of . . . misconduct."

Myrtle said, "Tippy, you actually saved the day. Philomena was trying to kill Puddin. She was the murderer all along."

Tippy stared at Myrtle as if she must have had a few glasses of wine. "Philomena? *Book club speaker* Philomena? Well, we certainly won't try out any of *your* suggestions."

At the mention of book club and at Tippy's acerbic tone, Philomena stirred and gingerly sat up. Her eyes flared with alarm and she moved as if to run away again.

Myrtle said, "Don't even think about it."

Puddin growled at Philomena as if to promise that her short, stubby legs would nevertheless overtake an injured Philomena if it came to it.

Erma swung her shovel at Philomena with feeling. Tippy stared at her through narrowed eyes. "Is that one of our gala props?" she demanded.

Erma blushed. "Wanda told me to meet her here at nine with something heavy. I thought we were taking selfies."

Miles frowned thoughtfully, looking down at the broken bottle. "And I came over to find your purse for the ginger ale Wanda mentioned. At precisely the same time."

Apparently, Wanda was able to tell time when it suited her. Myrtle said, "We should all be focusing on the fact that Philomena has murdered two people and tried to murder another."

"Yeah!" said Puddin, putting a hand to her throat and glaring at Philomena, who looked dully back at her. Puddin's other hand maintained a death grip on the takeaway bag of food.

"Do you have anything to say for yourself?" asked Myrtle.

Philomena didn't say anything.

Myrtle said, "Then allow me to fill in the awkward silence here while Miles goes to fetch the ambulance. It's too bad that your brother has to see you like this, but it can't be helped."

As Miles trotted off, Myrtle said, "You weren't as laid back about Amos ending your relationship as you made out. You've always been meticulous about your image in this town."

Puddin snorted. "Until you went around killin' people."

Myrtle gave her an impatient look. "Even then, Puddin. That's because Philomena never considered that she would get caught."

Tippy had carefully moved back from Philomena as if her depravity might be contagious.

Myrtle continued, "You see, Philomena was always a brainy child. More than bright—perhaps more than merely gifted. She was raised like an only child since her brother was born so much later than she was. Philomena was doted on by her parents. They made sure that she had everything she ever wanted."

"Spoilt!" hissed Puddin, who seemed to be getting even more worked up.

Wanda patted her pocket absently for a cigarette and then gave a dejected sigh when she remembered that she'd quit.

Erma said slowly, "So you mean that her parents set her up to think that she could *always* get what she wanted. And then, one day, she *didn't* get what she wanted!"

"Exactly," said Myrtle, although she was reluctant to encourage Erma. Encouraging Erma never led to anything good.

Tippy said doubtfully, "And she wanted Amos?" Her voice indicated that she'd never thought of Amos as very much of a catch.

Philomena's face was turning an unattractive shade of red. Myrtle had the feeling that of the people that Philomena most wanted to protect her reputation from, Tippy would rate high on the list.

Myrtle said, "Philomena and Amos actually had a good deal in common. For one thing, they were both intellectuals. For another, they enjoyed good books. And they liked to see plays and concerts and to travel. I'd imagine Philomena was very happy with Amos. Until he suddenly decided to go back to dating Alice. Then she knew she was going to have to punish him for that. It must have been even more of a slap to the face that it was *Alice* he was leaving her for and not someone else."

Erma frowned, looking much like a donkey in distress. "It made it look like he was sorry he stopped dating Alice! Like he was sorry he dated Philomena at all."

Tippy breathed, "So she sneaked over there and murdered him." She gaped, horrified, at Philomena.

"The library where Philomena worked is very close to Amos's house. She could easily have slipped over there, knocked Amos over the head with the glass bottle, and then slipped back to the library," said Myrtle. "What was more, she had some interesting knowledge. She knew that Puddin had had a public argument at the library with Amos over back pay. So there was a ready suspect after she murdered Amos."

Puddin spat out, "Sneaky!"

Myrtle shrugged. "She was taking a chance, considering that it was daylight, but think about it: no one would think it was odd that Philomena was there. As far as most people knew, they were still in a relationship. Philomena was careful not to bring in something that appeared to be a weapon, instead using a heavy object that was readily available inside the house. And Philomena was likely swift about it. How did it go, Philomena? Did you tell him off and then wait for him to turn his back on you to get some food and hit him?"

Philomena ended her silence. "I told him exactly what I thought of him. He didn't seem bothered about my opinion."

"Which only fueled the anger, I've no doubt. You hit him over the head and left to return for the library. You were so focused on getting away that you didn't realize that Puddin had spotted you as she'd arrived at Amos's house to clean," said Myrtle.

Puddin seemed to have gotten a sudden realization. "Hey, yeah! I saw *her*."

Myrtle said, "And maybe after word had gotten out that you'd discovered the body, Puddin, Philomena started thinking about it. Maybe you'd seen something."

Philomena said in a detached voice, "Or maybe she hadn't. It was hard to tell. And it had been a while before the police were called. She might have arrived much later after I'd left."

Myrtle said sharply, "But she hadn't. She'd merely taken the opportunity to watch her favorite game shows and slack off, completely unaware that Amos's body was in the kitchen."

Tippy gasped at the mental image of this tableau. Or perhaps she was gasping at that anyone had a favorite game show.

Philomena shifted on the ground and groaned. "Where is Steven?"

At that point they spotted Miles, not moving nearly as quickly now as he had when he'd trotted off in search of the ambulance. When he approached them he said, still breathing rather hard, "Another ambulance is on the way. Steven's ambulance had to transport someone to the hospital for a shellfish allergy." He gave Philomena a wary look as if she might leap savagely at them at any second. He stood back with Tippy.

Myrtle beamed at Miles. "We were walking through the murders with Philomena."

Philomena's glower indicated that Myrtle was taking more of a solo stroll.

Wanda prompted Myrtle. "Then Puddin showed off."

Puddin whipped her head around to frown at Wanda.

Myrtle said, "That's indeed the case. The town was buzzing that Puddin knew who the killer was. And Philomena didn't want to take the chance that it was true."

"It was a stupid thing to say," said Philomena icily.

Tippy said with a frown, "But what about Gabriel? Gabriel was attacked before Puddin was."

Myrtle said to Philomena, "You must have felt as if you were under siege from all sides, didn't you?"

Philomena shrugged. "Everyone seemed to know something. And I was unlucky. Gabriel had dropped by the library when I was at Amos's house. He asked for me at the circulation desk and was told I'd stepped out for a minute to make a phone call."

Myrtle nodded thoughtfully. "So you acted as if you were still going to be on the library grounds, in preparation for your alibi. But there was no phone call, of course. You'd stepped outside to rush to Amos's house. And Gabriel, when he stepped outside to look for you on the phone, never saw you."

Wanda croaked, "Bad luck. Or bad karma."

Myrtle continued, "Then Gabriel realized what it all meant when he learned that Amos had been murdered. He knew that Philomena didn't really have an alibi."

Tippy said, "And that she had a motive." She put her hand protectively to her throat as Philomena shot her a look.

Wanda said, "Then more bad luck."

Myrtle said, "More bad luck for Philomena *and* for Puddin. Puddin, you clearly must have happened upon Philomena at Gabriel's garage."

Puddin frowned suspiciously and Miles clarified, "You saw Philomena when you were at the garage."

Puddin looked defensive. "Didn't know I did."

"Well, I saw *you*," said Philomena with a snarl.

"Don't mean that I was payin' attention," said Puddin heatedly.

Miles said, "So Gabriel was blackmailing Philomena, then? Just as Amos was blackmailing him?"

Myrtle said slowly, "I don't somehow see Gabriel that way. I see him more as a big cat torturing a small, helpless creature."

"Except that I wasn't helpless," said Philomena. "And I wasn't in the mood to play games. He came by the library the day before the funeral and made all of these vague references right in front of other patrons."

"He enjoyed that, I bet," said Myrtle. "And then you started worrying about Puddin. Realizing she was also going to the gala, you looked for an opportunity to get her alone. Which she provided when she decided to go put her feet up for a while on a pool chaise and eat."

"Better than them loud speakers and no comfy seats," muttered Puddin.

The sound of an approaching emergency vehicle made them turn.

"The ambulance?" asked Philomena, looking hopeful.

"The police," said Myrtle succinctly.

Tippy sighed and brushed a miniscule speck from her immaculate white slacks. "I'm certainly glad it's over."

Philomena said, "I would have gotten away with it if it hadn't been for Puddin."

Puddin gave her a baffled look through narrowed eyes, having no idea how she had played any role in the proceedings whatsoever.

Myrtle said, "If *Wanda* hadn't led me to where you were attempting Puddin's murder, we wouldn't have had proof to take to the police. As it happens, we now have two excellent witnesses."

Wanda seemed to stand a bit taller as she grinned at Myrtle.

Red jogged up to their group with the ambulance arriving a couple of minutes later. He took Puddin aside first to interview and Myrtle could hear Puddin's animated account from yards away. Now that Puddin realized that she was off the hook for the murders, she was her old, sassy self again.

"An' I solved the case, too. That's why she wanted to kill me," said Puddin loudly.

Lieutenant Perkins arrived and he was speaking with Erma. Erma was also bragging about her exploits. "And I waved the shovel at Philomena. I could tell she thought it was all over. It reminded me of this time when I had this horrible stomach virus."

Myrtle sighed. Poor Lieutenant Perkins. First, he was speaking to Erma and then he was going to have to suspend his disbelief and interview Wanda.

Sloan appeared with his date some distance behind him. His eyes wide he mouthed, "You okay?" Myrtle nodded and mouthed, "My story." Sloan nodded and started taking pictures for the paper.

The gala was over and everyone was heading to their cars, craning their necks to figure out what was going on with the police cars, ambulance, golf cart, newspaper editor taking pictures, and assorted group of gala attendees. Finally, Red and Lieutenant Perkins questioned Myrtle. Puddin had fallen asleep by then, curled up in the golf cart.

Lieutenant Perkins listened attentively to Myrtle's story, carefully making notes. Red listened, too, although he made short, exasperated sounds whenever Wanda's name figured into the narrative. Perkins said at the end, "So, in your opinion, Amos was killed for revenge."

Myrtle said, "That's right. Because Philomena had always been babied. She'd always gotten her way. She couldn't handle rejection. And then Gabriel's death was all to protect her from discovery. Gabriel was determined to tease her with the information . . . he never planned on profiting from it. Instead, he found himself murdered."

Lieutenant Perkins nodded soberly. "Well, Mrs. Clover, I think that's all I have for you for tonight. I hope you can go home and get some rest. It's been a long night for you." A state policeman called him away and he added, "Excuse me."

Red said, "Mama, I hope you know that you had a lucky escape. Philomena was nobody to be messed with."

Myrtle said, "It seems to me that *Puddin* had the lucky escape. I was never in any danger." She paused. "Are you following me home tonight for some food? Unless you've succumbed to the uber-healthy diet?"

Red grinned. "No. Elaine has given up her healthy living agenda. She decided that the food was making me gain weight."

"Excellent!" said Myrtle. "Clearly she wasn't clued in that you were consuming full bags of potato chips at my house."

"Fingers crossed that the next hobby doesn't involve me at all," said Red.

Myrtle tapped Puddin, who continued snoring until Myrtle shook her by the shoulder. "Lemme go!" muttered Puddin without opening her eyes.

"It's time to go home," said Myrtle.

Miles and Wanda were already walking to the car as Puddin and Myrtle started slowly following them.

Miles drove to Puddin's house first. Puddin opened the car door and then turned to Wanda. "Thank you. I'm glad yer a witch."

Wanda gave her a tired smile and a wave as Puddin left.

Myrtle said, "Why don't you stay over at my house tonight, Wanda? It's a long drive home, after all. Besides, you wanted to watch the video of the lecture, didn't you? Or will Dan worry about you?"

Wanda gave a croaky laugh at the thought of her brother being concerned by her absence. "Nope. Sounds good."

Myrtle said, "Miles, you're not sleepy after all this, are you?"

He shook his head. "Exhausted, yes. Sleepy, no."

"Let's play our Scrabble game for a while then. Maybe that will settle us down. And I even have a few snacks in the house since Red hasn't been back to raid my kitchen," said Myrtle.

And that's what they did. Wanda curled up on the sofa with Miles's phone, watching the lecture and nodding to herself.

Miles and Myrtle faced off over the Scrabble table again. Myrtle gave a Cheshire cat smile. On her next move, she used tiles to spell out *victorious*.

About the Author

Elizabeth writes the Southern Quilting mysteries and Memphis Barbeque mysteries for Penguin Random House and the Myrtle Clover series for Midnight Ink and independently. She blogs at ElizabethSpannCraig.com/blog, named by Writer's Digest as one of the 101 Best Websites for Writers. Elizabeth makes her home in Matthews, North Carolina, with her husband. She's the mother of two.

Sign up for Elizabeth's free newsletter to stay updated on releases:

https://bit.ly/2xZUXqO

This and That

I love hearing from my readers. You can find me on Facebook as Elizabeth Spann Craig Author, on Twitter as elizabethscraig, on my website at elizabethspanncraig.com[1], and by email at elizabethspanncraig@gmail.com.

Thanks so much for reading my book...I appreciate it. If you enjoyed the story, would you please leave a short review on the site where you purchased it? Just a few words would be great. Not only do I feel encouraged reading them, but they also help other readers discover my books. Thank you!

Did you know my books are available in print and ebook formats? Most of the Myrtle Clover series is available in audio and some of the Southern Quilting mysteries are. Find the audiobooks here: https://elizabethspanncraig.com/audio/

Please follow me on BookBub for my reading recommendations and release notifications.

I'd also like to thank some folks who helped me put this book together. Thanks to my cover designer, Karri Klawiter, for her awesome covers. Thanks to my editor, Judy Beatty for her help. Thanks to beta readers Amanda Arrieta, Rebecca Wahr,

---

1. http://elizabethspanncraig.com/

Cassie Kelley, and Dan Harris for all of their helpful suggestions and careful reading. Thanks to my ARC readers for helping to spread the word. Thanks, as always, to my family and readers.

Other Works by Elizabeth

Myrtle Clover Series in Order (be sure to look for the Myrtle series in audio, ebook, and print):

Pretty is as Pretty Dies

Progressive Dinner Deadly

A Dyeing Shame

A Body in the Backyard

Death at a Drop-In

A Body at Book Club

Death Pays a Visit

A Body at Bunco

Murder on Opening Night

Cruising for Murder

Cooking is Murder

A Body in the Trunk

Cleaning is Murder

Edit to Death

Hushed Up

A Body in the Attic

Murder on the Ballot

Death of a Suitor

A Dash of Murder
Death at a Diner
A Myrtle Clover Christmas
Murder at a Yard Sale (2023)
Southern Quilting Mysteries in Order:
Quilt or Innocence
Knot What it Seams
Quilt Trip
Shear Trouble
Tying the Knot
Patch of Trouble
Fall to Pieces
Rest in Pieces
On Pins and Needles
Fit to be Tied
Embroidering the Truth
Knot a Clue
Quilt-Ridden
Needled to Death
A Notion to Murder
Crosspatch
Behind the Seams
Quilt Complex (2023)
The Village Library Mysteries in Order (Debuting 2019):
Checked Out
Overdue
Borrowed Time
Hush-Hush

Where There's a Will

Frictional Characters

Spine Tingling

A Novel Idea

End of Story

Memphis Barbeque Mysteries in Order (Written as Riley Adams):

Delicious and Suspicious

Finger Lickin' Dead

Hickory Smoked Homicide

Rubbed Out

And a standalone "cozy zombie" novel: Race to Refuge, written as Liz Craig